PASSING

REMARKS

PASSING REMARKS

HELEN HODGMAN

BALLANTINE BOOKS

NEW YORK

A Ballantine Book
Published by The Ballantine Publishing Group

http://www.randomhouse.com

Library of Congress Cataloging-in-Publication Data:
Hodgman, Helen.
Passing remarks / Helen Hodgman.—1st American ed.
p.   cm.
ISBN 0-345-41773-9 (alk. paper)
I. Title.
PR6058.O32P37   1998
823'.914—dc21   98-19968
                                                          CIP

Text design by Fritz Metsch
Cover design by Ruth Ross
Cover photographs by Abe Elshaikh

Manufactured in the United States of America

First American Edition: June 1998

10   9   8   7   6   5   4   3   2

Australian spelling and usage have been changed for the comfort of the American reader. Regrettably, there is nothing to be done about the unseasonable weather.

*J*ust imegine having your ectospasm running around william and nilliam among the unlimitless etha—gollah, it's imbillivibil.

— KRAZY KAT

*T*wo things happened to Rosemary early that summer: she won $30,000 playing keno at the Hakoah Club and she fell in love with a woman much younger than herself. Thus, laden with luck, she entered her fifty-first year.

Billie had started turning up at the beach, parking her motorbike in front of Rosemary's house. Sometimes she'd come with friends and sometimes she hadn't. On one such lone evening Billie found herself hassled by a landlocked lout with a hard-on who wanted to know where she got her muscles and her attitude. Billie was deciding what to do to him when a wild and curly wave delivered Rosemary to her feet. Seizing the moment, Billie held out her hand, raised her up and kissed her in a manner the boy and any others bobbing about like tea bags between the flags could not possibly mistake for sisterly.

Of course these dashing beginnings can take you different ways. It's all in the timing and in this case Billie had timed it right. Rosemary was bored. She was dull and sick of it, though the dullness had served its purpose by blunting those bits of desire left over after Lyn had gone back to America last year. She knew this new thing could cause her pain. It seemed like bad luck and it seemed like good luck. Why me? was the question she'd wanted to ask but didn't because in these heady zones it is better not to ask questions to which you do not already know the answers. They dispensed with ritual—that is to say, possibly, a lunch and the trading of recent sexual histories—they just walked back to Rosemary's place and did it.

From then on they met in secret. They met passionately. Rosemary grew thinner, neglected her friends, drank a bit too much, was permanently wet between her legs, and had never felt better in her life, or not for a long time anyway.

Then Billie didn't phone and didn't come round for a week, which was okay but then it was two weeks and it wasn't. In that fortnight Rosemary was supervising the renovations she was having done on her house thanks to her keno winnings and at work she was winding up her year. While she did these things she thought about what she knew about Billie—she'd dropped out of law at the end of her second year, was now working as a waiter at a cafe in Darlinghurst, and sang with a funk band sometimes.

Late one night the phone rang. She wanted Rosemary to come to this club she was at. She gave directions.

"Can't you come here?"

"No. Listen, just come, will you? We've got to talk."

"We can talk here."

"No."

Rosemary went. She parked and walked to the club. At the hole-in-the-wall entrance she paid the cover charge and the babydyke on the door wearing a T-shirt reading I CAME, I SAW, I'M BORED grabbed her hand and stamped her wrist.

"What does it say? Queer?"

"Only in certain lights," was the reply. Rosemary would have liked to inquire further into the meaning of this but she was anxious to find Billie. She wasn't at the bar. Try the packed dance floor. There she was, and she'd seen Rosemary. She'd caught the woman she was dancing with by the arm and pointed Rosemary out to her. The woman laughed. Rosemary smiled. She leaned against the wall and waited. She was fifty years old. She knew how to wait.

Billie and Rosemary sat at a table. Billie told Rosemary she'd stayed away because she'd wanted to be sure about what she wanted from this relationship. She wanted to wake up next to Rosemary in the morning quite often, see movies, go shopping with her, and meet her friends and if she couldn't have these things then clearly this thing wasn't going anywhere and they might as well stop it now.

"It doesn't have to stop," said Rosemary, and Billie took Rosemary's hand and led her to a dark room, to a mattress on the floor where Billie whispered, "Darling, raise your hips," so her lips and tongue could provide the pleasure they both sought.

•

Rosemary sometimes wonders, when she's alone in the house, just who the unfamiliar middle-aged woman is, glimpsed crossing the empty room when night turns windows to mirrors—just who is in this bag of skin?

She picks up a gold-topped jar and begins to prepare her face for her New Year's Eve party. Her life and her house are in order. Billie is sleeping in Rosemary's bed in this room at this moment and all is prepared in the kitchen—nothing complicated, a few simple and delicious things bought at the fish market that morning and prepared this afternoon with the help of the Japanese cookbook her friend Gin had given her for Christmas. She is particularly pleased with the squid and asparagus lightly dressed with a mustard-miso sauce and arranged in petite portions on the fine shell-shaped plates she's so fond of.

Rosemary puts down the jar and smooths her neck and the skin beneath her chin with the back of her hand. She applies her makeup. She does so slowly. It is not a thing she does every day, but when she does she enjoys it. She hopes it holds. These days after a few drinks her face tends to turn pink and blotchy and fall apart.

Kristeva tumbles from the bookcase where she has been busily punishing some innocent thing with her claws. She looks to see if Rosemary has seen, then stalks across the room to hide herself in the folds of the muslin curtain falling softly to the floor.

Billie opens her eyes and watches Rosemary and decides she's never been this happy, not ever. She remembers times when she was little and watched her mother getting ready to go out, making up her face in exactly the absorbed manner Rosemary is employing now. She had been really small then, in the days before her mother turned into a hippie and eschewed all beauty products because they were made from whales or whatever.

"You look gorgeous."

Rosemary turns. "Do I?"

Billie gets up, goes to Rosemary, kisses her lightly on her freshly lipsticked lips. "Don't want to spoil your makeup."

Rosemary tells her that basically she doesn't care if Billie smears her makeup all over the walls and tears her limb from limb but on the other hand they *are* expecting guests.

"Of course we are," says Billie. "They'll be here soon, won't they, all your friends?"

"And yours." Rosemary imagines these friends of Billie's sanding down their broomsticks, shining up their leather, polishing their spurs in readiness for the night. Sewing last-minute sequins on Fruit of the Loom underpants. Swallowing Ecstasy pills and waiting for the bliss to kick in. Rosemary only hopes that, having gone to so much trouble, they won't get lost on the way. Billie's friends tended to become sullen and confused when summoned to the eastern suburbs from their covens in the inner west. It was too hard, too far, and, worse, too bourgeois, though Rosemary doesn't think that is the word they'd use. She doesn't know what word they'd use but they'd made it clear how they felt. Such a spiky lot they were, in both opinion—when you could wheedle one out of them—and appearance. What would her friends make of Billie's friends and what would Billie make of hers?

"JoJo's riding my bike over." Billie keeps her surfboards, wetsuits, and flippers at Rosemary's but has left her motorbike behind with her friend JoJo in Glebe. No point keeping it at the beach to rust, and Billie doesn't ride it in the city much, preferring to use public transport or to borrow Rosemary's car.

"Sometimes, like just now, you remind me of my mother," says Billie.

"Your mother? How?"

"Can't explain exactly. You know. It was just a feeling I had, watching you."

Something's happening in Rosemary's stomach. She knows there's pain on its way. Some great black music mistress is already setting it to music in her head—*Dere's a great pain a-comin', Lawd Lawd.*

As careless Billie leaves the room to shower, Rosemary, in several seconds of surrealist license brought about by shock, knows the angel of death has entered in and stands firmly in her landscape with feet apart, arms akimbo, wings furled.

Those dark wings have, unsummoned, brushed by Rosemary before as they brush by everyone in the course of a life. Rosemary has had close encounters on the following occasions: at a school swimming carnival when she was seven, on a wet November night in Ontario in 1978 when a car tire blew, and eight years before that on a houseboat moored on the River Thames near Oxford, and lastly, diving the Cod Hole up on the Great Barrier Reef four years ago. And there was one time she doesn't remember because, unlike those other times, she hadn't known what was happening in the singles bar in Tacoma where death had curled close and gibbered in her face in the form of a serial killer who'd bought her a drink and then decided he didn't want her because her accent threw him.

For its part, the angel knows tonight is another false alarm. It is often summoned to attend by a chance remark that has brought fear and loss bubbling to the top. It is content to simply eavesdrop while the crocodile nibbles of anxiety turn into full-blown bloody bites. *She could leave me for someone else.*

No one, in all Rosemary's years of practicing serial monogamy, has ever left her for someone else. She has left them. Sympathetically, supportively, and even, on one occasion, not until after they'd endured several couples-counseling appointments that surely proved that she and the lover in question were serious, caring people who both really wanted it to work and therefore could walk away with neither one feeling guilty. Rosemary conveniently forgets those with whom it wasn't like that at all, the ones who still snarl and lash out beyond the pale of memory. She remains proud of the fact that several of her lovers are now friends and even those who aren't don't gag at the sight of her when she bumps into them at the theater or somewhere.

She could leave me for someone younger.

Let's face it, Rosemary, the whole world's younger than you are. Look at them teeming about out there. Even the prime minister's younger than you are—not by much, it's true, but every second counts.

She could leave me for someone younger and therefore more attractive.

Exactly. Thank you. That's it—someone more attractive and less like her mother.

Rosemary goes to the glass doors. She opens them and steps onto a narrow balcony with a small bridge at one end. Kristeva unwraps herself from the curtains and joins her. The angel follows cautiously. It is not fond of gardens. They cause people to dawdle on this earth longer than they otherwise might. God only knows what people get up to in them, right from that first recorded fuck onward. Rosemary presses a switch and a small, densely planted garden clicks into focus beyond the bridge. Red impatiens glow like coals in the dark and white ones float cool and luminous. Jasmine foams over the side fences and the shadows of the kentia palms flow pleasingly across the lime-washed walls.

Lauren the electrician has done a good job with the outdoor lighting, and the indoor lighting too, come to that. Rosemary hopes she'll turn up tonight, but Lauren hadn't been sure she could, had thought perhaps her lover could have other plans for New Year's. She said she'd ring and let Rosemary know, but she hasn't.

Rosemary liked having Lauren round the house. Her light efficient presence had come as a relief after the leaden good cheer of the male builders who'd been there for months. But mostly she'd enjoyed her feelings of speculative lust as she watched Lauren climbing ladders in her short frayed cutoffs, the work boots she wore making incongruously heavy punctuation marks at the end of her long legs. Then Rosemary thinks of Billie's legs wrapped round her as they'd been less than one hour ago, and death, foiled by gardening, sex, and the impending company of friends, unfurls its wings and departs.

·

Alan will be the first to arrive. He's always either early or late because he doesn't have a car and public transport always lands him on one side or the other of the appointed hour, never quite on target. He complains constantly about the vagaries of buses and ferries but for some reason has never learned to drive.

Rosemary walks along the hallway to the linen cupboard. Poor Alan, she thinks, in the manner of one who has found love toward one who has not. She takes out a pile of beach towels. After midnight everyone would go over to the beach to swim in the rock pool. As a favor to Rosemary nobody swims in the surf. Rosemary doesn't want anyone's drugged or drunken drowning on her conscience.

Would Billie's friends join them or would they prefer to stay behind and wreck the place? Rosemary can't believe she's thought that. What is the matter with her? She's been getting strange about lots of things lately—for instance, those boys you see everywhere wearing baseball caps backward make her furious. Didn't they know how stupid they looked? She wants to rip them off their heads and make them eat them.

The doorbell. Rosemary hugs Alan and kisses his cheek. Kristeva rolls at his feet on the rose-colored Chinese rug.

"I hate cats, especially designer cats." Alan pokes Kristeva with his foot as she rolls and purrs and clutches at his shoe. "You have been busy. The place is looking wonderful. Very swish."

"My brother's term for it is Hollywood kitsch."

"That sounds like him. Poor Richard."

"He's all right."

"You have mellowed. Must be all this material comfort."

"Must be."

Rosemary feels the slight snag of jealousy behind her friend's words tugging at her. Rosemary knows their father's death lies behind her more positive feeling for her older brother. It has removed the need for the two of them to compete for his attention. Rosemary does not say this, though on another occasion she might because Alan is a good friend and interested in these things.

"It's been my lucky year" is all she says.

Rosemary looks round her beautiful room with a sense of unease. Good luck. Bad luck. What did it mean? Was there a price to be paid for everything? She's old enough to be Billie's mother. Billie herself had said so, or something very like it.

"How's the child?" asks Alan with a smirk he probably sees as a smile. Can he read her mind?

Car doors are slamming outside in the street, there is a chattering on the stairs. This is about to be a party.

"Here we go," says Alan, popping the first champagne cork of the evening.

.

*R*osemary has found her first gray pubic hair. She removes it with her eyebrow tweezers, walks to the window, opens it, and releases the hair, which drifts away in the direction of the cafe two doors up the road and comes to gentle rest on the focaccia with marinated artichoke hearts, salami, olive paste, and the ubiquitous sun-dried tomatoes sitting on an outside table.

The day bounces in. Sharp street noises and sea sounds. The sea is big this morning. Waves topple, big as apartment houses. Container ships line up on the horizon like targets in a shooting gallery. The long deep waves are shredded by surfers trailing rainbow plumes. Rosemary watches them, delighted as always by the transformation of those landlocked and horrible louts into a graceful race apart when they hit the beach like warriors in their multicolored rubber suits, firing their hot buttered boards across the churning water and flaying their way out through the foam.

It had been a good party. "The best yet," as Alan had said, first to arrive and last to leave, dancing across the pavement toward the waiting cab, an arm round each of them. Rosemary was pleased Alan and Billie had got on well, despite Alan's claim that he really couldn't take anyone born in the seventies seriously. Rosemary was amused to note that Alan had updated himself a bit; it used to be anyone born in the sixties, and before that it was anyone born in the second half of the twentieth century.

"By the way, girls," Alan had yelled, sticking his head out the window as the cab drove off, "I'm getting a car. Just decided. New Year's resolution! G'bye."

"I'm not making any resolutions," Billie had said. "At least not until I get back."

In the phone booth outside the house a very large and sweaty Pacific Islander had bellowed "Happy New Year" into the phone.

"Back?"

"Broken. Broken. Broken," sobbed the Islander. Rosemary wondered if it was the phone he referred to, or his heart. He vomited into the mouthpiece and Rosemary immediately lost interest in the state of his heart. She also vowed she would never use that or any public phone again.

"Back from where?"

"I know I should've told you before. I wanted to, but I didn't know how."

"Never mind. Tell me now."

"I'm going away. For a few weeks. As much time as I need. I'm not sure." Cockroaches, big as park benches, were holding meetings in the gutter.

"Who with?"

"Not with anyone. I'm going away to think about what I do next. The last two years have been a bit of a mess for me. I mean, I've had a good time. A great time, really. But, you know, I've got to think about the future."

"I'll miss you."

"I'll miss you too. You know I will."

"You'll phone, won't you? Send me a postcard or something?"

Billie drew Rosemary closer. They kissed.

"Filthy fucking lezzos," the man in the phone booth screamed.

Rosemary had wanted to cry. She'd closed her eyes so she wouldn't. She'd heard the man thrashing around in the phone booth. She'd heard the door burst open, seen him stagger toward Billie's motorbike parked at the curb. He reached out his hand to touch it. Bad move. Billie had had him on his back in seconds, his arm pinned at the wrist by her boot, his fingers waving on the far side like so much disconnected spaghetti. "Aaargh!" he'd screamed. "Aaarghaaaarrrggghhhh!" and then Rosemary had opened her eyes to find no such scene. The man was lurching his way across the road to the bus stop. Billie was watching him go.

"Poor dude," she'd said, and Rosemary had felt ashamed. Where she'd seen a base brute in a tasteless shirt, Billie had seen a fellow human being adrift in a merciless world, a puppet jerked about by forces about as far beyond his influence as the planet Pluto. A man who, thanks to people like Rosemary's forebears, was a shattered victim of the postcolonial experience. But what, Rosemary had cried to herself as she so often does, what can *I* do about it?

Back in the bright morning she sits on the wide ledge of the window looking out over the orange lids of those phone booths. Across the road to the beach is the park with its miniature train and its coin-in-the-slot barbecues and those mad shelters with conical roofs dotted all across the grass. Separating the fringe of the park from the street itself is a sunken roadway where buses end their journey from Central Station and wait until it's time to go back again.

The skin cancer people are setting up their information tent on the beach. The Surf Watch guy, whom Rosemary knows vaguely because he hangs out at the cafe up the road when he isn't measuring the degrees of crap in the ocean, trolls along the beach with his glass container on a piece of string, stopping now and then to poke at the sand with one end of a ballpoint pen and then write something on his clipboard with the other end. Rosemary just hopes he's never stuck the wrong end in his mouth. She'd asked him once what he was looking for.

"Grease balls, condom rings, and panty liners."

It should be enough to put you off swimming in the sea for life but somehow it isn't.

The mobile police station enters the park and backs into position beside the surf club. The beach is a complicated place these days, thinks Rosemary, as she sips her orange juice and hopes that the thin drill of pain she'd woken up with behind her left eye will wear itself out by afternoon. Perhaps a swim might help. Billie has already gone over to the beach for one. Rosemary decides analgesics are easier, then, remembering the anti-inflammatories her doctor prescribed when she hurt her back last year, she goes in search of the bottle and takes the two pills left in it plus three Panadol capsules, which should achieve something.

Where's Billie? Rosemary hopes she hasn't been caught in the rip, stepped on a needle, or slipped on a panty liner. To

Rosemary, perched above it, the world looks full of unease this morning. The phone booth is full of vomit, the sea is full of crap, the park is full of people, and Billie is going away. She watches vast extended families struggle across the grass toward the barbecues carrying what looks like half the furniture they own as well as a lot of things Rosemary considers unhealthy to eat and drink.

Just below the window, next to the pedestrian crossing, two motorists prepare to die over the last illegal parking spot in the street. The people in the car that has gained the space cower inside as the driver of the unsuccessful vehicle and his passengers pile out and begin to kick and rock it. Three children cry in the backseat. Rosemary wonders where these people have come from and why they are willing to risk their children's mental health over a place to park the car. Made pious by the pain in her head, she asks herself whatever has happened to the idea of the redemptive life.

Tim, her neighbor who teaches leisure-craft design part-time at a community college, comes out of his house and leads his small, bandy son Sam across the road to the park. Tim is leading a campaign for residential parking. Rosemary doesn't think this is a good idea. She hadn't gone to the concerned residents' meeting and she hadn't signed their petition to council because she didn't think that it would stop people parking where they wanted to anyway, and then everyone would just get doubly indignant when someone parked in their place. She'd talked to the local shopkeepers and they didn't want it either. They depended on visitors to the beach being able to park within reach of the shops. They couldn't depend on the custom of the residents, who did their shopping at the supermarkets, though the little shops were handy for the morning papers and when they ran out of milk. The busy summer weekends and the school holidays were the foundation of their livelihood.

Rosemary's tongue finds the funny place on her bottom lip that bothers her from time to time—a small rough patch that won't go away. A legacy, no doubt, of her own endless childhood summers in the days when sunshine was good for you and her mother's constant weary cry had been "Why don't you children go and play *outside*," and hats were what grown-ups wore to horse races and weddings. She must get this lip checked. She can't understand why she keeps putting it off. Not wanting to know the truth was not like her. She belonged to the wrong socioeconomic group for such self-neglect.

Now Billie's coming back from the beach, crossing the park, stepping lightly through the flowing tide of the laden. She vanishes behind the buses parked at the terminus and reappears to climb the steps up to the street and now she's here, damp, salty, kissing Rosemary's neck.

Tomorrow morning Billie will be leaving to drive up the coast to visit her mother, who lives in a place Rosemary has not previously heard of called Bundagen. Then she is going on to Byron Bay to stay, perhaps even to work for a while, with a friend of hers who runs a resort up there. This friend is something of a mentor to Billie, it seems, though Billie's never mentioned her before. There's a possibility too, of Billie's going farther north, perhaps as far as Cairns. Nothing was definite. It depended on the travel plans of a Dutch girl, the cousin of a boy Billie had become friends with during an exchange visit to Holland when she was at school.

"Is there anything you have to do today?" asks Billie. "Anyone coming round? Anyone we have to see? Or can we spend the day in bed?"

The phone rings. "I shouldn't have said anything."

The answering machine comes on, but whoever it is doesn't choose to leave a message. Rosemary remembers she'd made an arrangement last night to see a film this afternoon with Sara and Susan. She'll phone, put them off until Billie has gone. Rosemary goes cold, takes her hand from Billie's breast.

"What's the matter?" But Rosemary cannot tell Billie she is scared of being alone, not necessarily in the immediate future but in the longer term. Old and alone. Ill and lonely. This morning it seems possible people she'd always dismissed as pathetic have a point. Stay married and live longer. Stay together and live. They'd be printing it on bumper stickers next. Rosemary tells herself to stop it. You get a cat and you cope, Rosemary tells herself firmly. Or a dog, if you must. A dog is always so pleased to see you when you get home from work. What she needs is a drink. She knows alcohol is a depressant, but, quite honestly, in the short term at least, it does the trick. Luckily, there's still a bottle of champagne in the fridge. She opens it, hands a glass to Billie.

"To your travels," she says, and drinks.

"Cheers, lover," says Billie. And Rosemary reminds herself she'd rather be dead than totter handcuffed and in tandem toward the grave.

Rosemary phones Sara and Susan, and Billie goes to bed to wait for her. When she strips off her bathing suit, bits of beach fly everywhere. Billie does her best to brush it away. She knows Rosemary's bound to notice, but she doesn't, or if she does she doesn't complain because sand on the sheets is as nothing compared to the thorn of self-doubt in her flesh. Instead Rosemary, legs spread, finds herself thinking she ought to have a pap smear soon because it has been too long since she had one. Billie looks up, smiles her shiny heart-stopping smile.

"It's gone. Your little silver hair. It was so pretty. I loved it."

Rosemary wonders why Billie loved it. She wants to know if this too reminds Billie of her mother, but she doesn't like to ask.

They watch the weather forecast at the end of the seven o'clock news, Rosemary wishing silently that there would be no rain anywhere on the map because her head is filled with bleak skids and the bruised chrome of motorbikes spinning out in the rain.

.

Billie zooms along the turnpike headed for Newcastle and the north, thinking about yesterday afternoon and last night and Rosemary. Billie thinks of all those dreary crushes her friends have had and indeed still have on older women, all hot, unreciprocated, and ultimately shaming, and here she was adored, accepted, sexual, and secure in the arms of experience. Not that it was always easy. Sometimes Billie felt unsure. Times like the party when she was about to be faced with the ranks of Rosemary's friends, the heads of blue ribbon committees—there were lots of those going on—the doctors, the lawyers, the artists, academics, and such, and all she could do was stand staring at the heap of clothes in front of her and panic about what to wear. What would they be wearing? The committee members, for instance. Did they wear shoulder pads to parties or only to lunch? For all she knew, they wore them to bed as well. She could see them all lined up toothless and mumbling on the verandah of some future rest home for faded femocrats, scrawny arms flung wide to illustrate their quavering claims that, once, they'd worn shoulder pads *this* big.

Billie had finally plucked a black miniskirt and halter top from her pile, found her only pair of fuck-me pumps, greased back her hair, reinserted her nose stud, and gone to join the party. Only to be met, challenged, by two pairs of cold eyes—two green, two blue, and which belonged to Susan and which belonged to Sara, Billie couldn't give a fuck. They'd been cooing around the kitchen admiring the blue terrazzo work surfaces when Rosemary led Billie over to introduce her. Their united gaze, it had seemed to Billie, said Rosie's new kitchen was a dream but her new lover was a serious breach of taste.

"Billie. *Billie.* Is it short for Wilhelmina?"

Billie had been named after an English actress her mother

admired. Billie thought it an excellent name, though she'd had a few hassles with it along the way, at school, for example. That sort of overt stuff she could deal with, but the kind of icy rubbish these two were handing out was not so simple. How would Rosemary have taken it if she'd started hurling her scrawny mates all around the kitchen in time-honored playground fashion?

Billie told them her mother had picked the name the second Billie'd popped out into the world and the doctor scooped her up and said, "Congratulations, it's a bonny bouncing lesbian!" Billie had watched the fine creases of confusion that constituted Sara's and Susan's faces slowly arrange themselves into tight and tidy smiles before they turned their minds back to higher things—whether or not it was really necessary to install a bidet, the conclusion being yes it was, absolutely. Talk of interior decoration bored Billie. Rosemary was always poring over copies of *Vogue Living*, *Interiors*, and so on. Once Billie had found Rosemary in the bath reading a copy of *Vogue Interiors* that featured a special supplement on kitchens.

"Oooh. House porn!" she'd whispered, lifting her skirt and rubbing herself to make her point, and Rosemary had pulled her into the bath and finished the job for her while European cooktops and automatic icemakers drowned around them.

·

Billie's mother, who waits for her at the end of this long road, does not have money and neither does Billie yet, but she intends to. Billie's mother foolishly clings to hippiedom well into middle age, and has no money and no phone, though she does have a bashed-up Holden Kingswood pickup truck. She also has had in her life a succession of men she refers to as "my old man," which sounded strange to Billie once but sounds less so now since the phrase has become literally true of those old men with scraggly gray ponytails.

Billie mulls over this question of money and her own mother's attitude toward it. It didn't do to be casual about money. Billie couldn't understand how any woman would willingly embrace powerlessness, but her mum seemed almost proud of the fact. "I'm a bit of a sixties person," she'd say, as if this was something to boast about.

Money equals power and freedom, thinks Billie, but there must be other ways of getting it other than clawing your way toward the light shining through the glass ceiling inside some male institution. Billie doesn't want equal opportunity, Billie wants a different planet.

In her last two years at high school two diseases had been rampant among bright young women: anorexia nervosa and the desire to be a lawyer. Law hadn't been a long-term ambition of Billie's but, when her high school grades were high enough to make it an option, she'd chosen it and found it easy and mechanical once she got the knack of it.

In her second year she hadn't gone to class at all. Instead she'd gone to Uganda with her lover, Robin, who had been making a documentary on AIDS. There, in a village in the north, they'd found an old woman with magical powers who'd dug a big hole in the ground and set up shop as an AIDS treatment center. All who came were given a mouthful of dirt and sent away. Not so very different from our own system, thinks Billie. She slides in a Madonna cassette and turns up the volume. Billie loves having Madonna inside her helmet.

No cops around that she can see. She eases the throttle. Vroom. Zoom. Wind whips the laughter from Billie's lips. Go for it, Billie. Let's go.

•

Rosemary phones the pest control company and makes a time for next week to have the place done. Cleaning up after the party she'd found a family of those small light brown cockroaches in the microwave.

"German, they are," says the man on the phone, which makes Rosemary all the more eager to wipe them out.

She drives out to the university not because she absolutely has to—Rosemary resolutely refused to teach any summer courses this year—but to pick up her chair and see what her friend Daphne is up to.

She takes the smelly lift down to the bottom floor of the sociology department and begins walking along the corridor. As always, half the lights are out, their bulbs broken or missing. Not much is happening down here in the dungeon, though the car park had been almost full and she'd recognized the cars of several of her colleagues.

A strong smell of cigarette smoke coming from under a firmly closed door tells her Daphne is at work in her room on the windowless side of the corridor. On this door is pinned a sign reading EVERYWHERE WOMEN ARE REDISCOVERING THE GODDESS. Had someone given it to her for Christmas? Did Daphne come out of there for Christmas? Rosemary wasn't sure. She didn't come out for New Year's Eve; every year Rosemary asked her and every year she refused. Someone could've burrowed along the tunnel and pinned the sign on as a surprise. Well, at least, thinks Rosemary, as she searches for the key to her own door, Daphne will never have to worry about skin cancer.

The room is stuffy, full of thick yellow light. The book shelves are overflowing. Cartons of books and papers stacked against the wall wait for her to do something about them. In the corner, partly hidden by the door, is a heap of periodicals from all over the world. Brittle and yellowing, unread.

She checks her messages, none of which matter. She angles the blinds to cut the glare and pushes a chair across to the window and sits in it a minute looking at the dust-coated native plants that flourish in the defaced concrete planter boxes that define the disgraceful area described by whatever company of morons designed this place as the lower quadrangle. Rosemary spins in her chair to face the fire hazard behind the door. What to do about it?

Rosemary used to read all these, every one and every word, but now she doesn't because the more she reads the more she keeps getting the feeling that this is where she came in. So much for those who cannot remember the past being condemned to repeat it—what about those who remember the past all too well and are still condemned to repeat it? There they all are, peeping out from behind the door, all the old issues—equal opportunity, equal pay, abortion, censorship, capital punishment, racism, sexism. Why should Rosemary spend what remains of her life—and from the way that funny bit on her lip seems to be spreading, that may well be not so long—watching these people trampling through the well-worn thickets of déjà vu to reach a forest of foregone conclusions? Better just take her chair and go.

But first, Daphne.

Rosemary goes to her door. Knocks. A scuffling sound, then silence. Rosemary opens the door. Daphne is crouched, gray and feral, among her spilling ashtrays.

"What do you want?"

Actually Rosemary would like a hand with her chair but knows any such request is doomed to failure.

"Nothing."

"Well, what are you doing here then?"

"Well, I just thought . . . if there's anything—you know—anything I can do, just . . ." Rosemary's voice sinks in the swamp of an unlikely list of things she could do for Daphne.

"Oh, I see. Well, there isn't. Thanks." Very grudging, this last. Oh, go fuck yourself, thinks Rosemary, smiling politely as she closes the door, picks up her chair, and goes home to see how the cockroaches are spending their last days.

·

Billie sits in a Kmart parking lot. She's just come off her motorbike going round the traffic circle in front of the Big Banana in Coffs Harbour, which has given her a fright. She sits trying to regulate her breathing, and, as people stream past her, she finds herself dwelling on the distressing amount of underwear that must exist in the world and where it all goes to in the end.

Her grandmother, Billie remembers, used to boil her worn-out knickers and use them for dustrags. Do people still do that? Billie feels sure that no one these days waits for their underwear to become threadbare before discarding it, though her knowledge of the subject is patchy. Billie's mother has no time for underwear and neither does Billie except for a small collection specially chosen for seductive purposes that she'd left at home.

Possibly because she's not had the underwear to do it with, Billie's mother has never dusted anything, saying that a bit of dust never hurt anyone and once the full complement of dust has gathered in anyone's house, it does not increase. Billie quite likes the fuzziness and the sensation of soft landings this policy gives to the spaces round her mother. Before she'd moved in with Rosemary, Billie had dusted some things but not others, usually using her sleeve, dirty T-shirts waiting to go to the laundromat, or anything else at hand. Rosemary used a feather duster for her books and the cedar blinds in her study and Mr. Sheen and various soft yellow cloths for everything else except the dining table, for which she used a special wax made in Tasmania.

Rosemary claimed that for her housework was a form of meditation. Billie thought this a fairly insufferable remark. Through an advertisement in *Lesbians on the Loose* Rosemary had found The Dirty Girls, who came in and took care of the windows and floors and the bathroom. Rosemary had decided it was all right to use women to do your dirty work as long as they were lesbian because presumably they weren't doing it from a position of oppression. Considering how much they charged, Billie supposes Rosemary is right.

She picks up her helmet, stands, stretches. Old shoppers eye her curiously. Billie does her best not to see them. She can't bear the way they look; the men creaking along like wrecked vinyl armchairs in shorts with their bowed legs knotted with veins and whorls of misshapen cartilage. Gnarled gryphons' toes throttle rubber thongs. Billie avoids their watery eyes and tries not to see the bloody glowworms of capillaries clustered on cheeks and noses.

I'll never be that age, vows Billie. It can't happen to me. I'll die first. Billie didn't dare look at the women. The men were bad enough, but they were only men after all and so didn't matter so much.

Billie thinks these things and feels ashamed. She tells herself that there is more to them than the decay that meets the eye; that these old ruined people have rich inner lives or something. But she doesn't believe it.

·

*T*here is an hour at the end of every summer's day at the beach when a particular light touches all things, the world turns luminous, and beauty is difficult to ignore no matter who gets in the way. The perfect evening stretches to the horizon, and a high sweet singer in the street below starts up:

> ". . . *to love mankind it is our duty,*
> *but I adore your simple beauty."*

Rosemary stops reading, and Kristeva, who has been relentlessly stalking back and forth along the bookshelves, stops to listen and to stretch.

Rosemary goes to the window but finds no sign of the unlikely singer, only a skateboarder thrashing by—one of those boys you only find at the beach or in an old Australian cartoon, the raucous orange-colored freckly kind with no eyelashes who were never that amusing to begin with. Rosemary has a rare moment of penis envy—if she had one, she'd whip it out and piss on that head, oblivious as a bullet. Instead she feeds the grumbling Kristeva, changes into a dress she'd bought to cheer herself up when she was stuck in Wagga Wagga for a week two years ago for some unremembered academic reason, switches on the burglar alarm and the answering machine, then goes down to her car and drives to Oxford Street in search of color and movement and to do a bit of shopping. She buys two world music CDs from Folkways Records and several bunches of lilies from the Loyal Florist. She puts these flowers carefully on the backseat of her car and drives to Taylor Square.

•

Billie stops, gets gas, decides to use the restroom. Yuck. Mistake. She should've just stopped on the road and gone behind some bushes. She turns to leave. The door opens. A woman stands there. About to enter, she hesitates. Her eyes travel from Billie to the female sign on the door and back again. She compares this painted blob in a skirt to Billie, who doesn't conform to this signifier of female gender. Since the woman too wears what she would probably refer to as slacks, there must be more to her doubt than Billie's lack of a skirt.

Deciding she is in the wrong place, she leaves. Billie washes her hands, remembering another washroom—Singapore Airport—and a woman, fractious child on hip, whose gaze had caught and held. The woman's lustful, casual glance conveyed a message writ backward in the mirror neither she nor Billie was in a position to answer but which each had understood.

"To come out is to say that we come," she tells her reflection in the crooked fly-blown mirror, and, though she doesn't know exactly what she means, she's pleased with it.

•

Rosemary stands in front of the rows of dyke books at the back of the shop. All the faggot books are closer to the door. Faggots, being a branch of men, have more money and perhaps it is only fitting that they not have to walk so far to spend it.

Rosemary is unsure how she feels about the books she's standing in front of. Billie buys these books all the time, and Rosemary has read a few. They are badly written and soppy and the dykes she knows aren't like the ones who strut these pages. They do not go round town tracking down murderers and solving mysteries, mainly, Rosemary supposes, because there aren't many mysteries that come their way and also, as any sane dyke—or for that matter, any sane woman of any persuasion—knows, murderers are far more likely to track you down than you are them.

It reminds Rosemary of the Nancy Drew books and how in her last year at school she had written her own Nancy Drew book called *Nancy Goes on the Pill*. She'd left the manuscript on a streetcar in Melbourne the weekend she went there to have an abortion, telling her mother she was staying at a girlfriend's place and telling her boyfriend nothing at all. She'd paid for it out of her summer job money. Rosemary cannot think, as she stands here some decades later, why she had taken the manuscript to Melbourne with her in the first place.

Billie, who has never heard of Nancy Drew and has never found it necessary to concern herself with birth control, had said that the quality or otherwise of the writing wasn't the point. It is a good and self-affirming thing to read these books because they have a positive attitude toward being queer that counteracts all the negative flak coming at you from everywhere. In her case, stuck in a heterosexist high school, the availability of such books had saved her the trouble of believing she had to prove anything to anyone by having a boyfriend and trying to pass as straight.

"Hi, Rosemary."

Who was this? Rosemary, ever hopeless with names, flounders politely. Who this is, is Valentine Smith, lover of Lauren the electrician, who had, in fact, come to Rosemary's party after all.

"Good party," says Val. "Good book," she adds, plucking something off the shelf and handing it to Rosemary.

Rosemary opens the good book while Valentine collects any free publication she can find because she's on her way to visit a friend in the AIDS ward at St. Vincent's and hasn't any money to buy an improper book, due to being on unemployment.

Blaize checked her rearview mirror again. The red Mercedes convertible had been following for miles. It had swung in behind her as she'd left her office in Hollywood and headed out along Sunset Boulevard toward the beach. Blaize guessed the woman at the wheel to be in her early twenties. She had short curly blond hair, wore Ray Bans, and had a state-of-the-art car stereo that Blaize could hear when they stopped at the lights. The woman's lips and nail polish matched the finish on her car.

That was all the information she had to go on, but she was so used to sizing women up that she automatically imagined the kind of body this one would have and she liked it.

"Don't follow me unless you mean it, sugar," said Blaize.

Rosemary pictures herself pulling out from the parking lot at the university and lustfully fixing the car ahead of her in her sights. She pulls alongside this car and gives its short-haired, Ray-Banned driver the once-over—cool Rosemary with her heavy-lidded, appraising eyes and her take-it-or-leave-it attitude. And in this case, Rosemary ruefully concludes, it would prove to be a case of leave it since the car would almost certainly turn out to be a white Volvo with one of those BABY ON BOARD signs stuck to the back window.

"Are you going to Max and Annie's commitment ceremony on Saturday?"

Max and Annie are members of the Mountain Lesbian News collective. Rosemary met them when she went along to a biweekly Friends of Dorothy evening after finding a flyer advertising this group pushed under the door in a plain brown envelope one Friday night when she'd driven up late from town. Max had seen Rosemary walking down the street and decided to flush her out.

"I'm never wrong," she'd crowed when Rosemary walked cautiously into the Women's Resource Center in Katoomba, where these gatherings are held.

"No, I don't think . . ." Rosemary remembers the gold embossed card inviting her to the ceremony lying unRSVP'd on the kitchen table up in Leura. "I don't really know Max and Annie."

"I think you should come. I think everyone should support such an affirming event. It's important for the community. And you've got a place up there, haven't you? So you'll be there anyway."

Although weddings have never been Rosemary's favorite form of party, she feels robbed of excuses by her undeniable proximity to the undeniably affirming event and finds herself saying she'll be there. A certain shyness, which is nothing to be proud of in a woman her age, gives her a sinking feeling in the pit of her stomach even as she says it. She wonders what form such a ceremony might take.

"Well, see you then, then," says Valentine, adding the gay gossip sheets *Sydney Star Observer* and *Capital Q* to her pile of freebies and exiting before Rosemary can think to ask her whether or not she should take Max and Annie a commitment gift. Rosemary decides she will. Rosemary is hungry and her thoughts naturally stray toward cookbooks and dinner. She puts the book she's holding back on the shelf and then, because she wants to know how Blaize makes out with the woman in the car, she takes it off again.

"Good book," says the girl behind the counter.

"So I'm told," says Rosemary.

"Sexy," says the girl, and Rosemary, to her dismay, finds herself blushing. What is the matter with her and why is the world suddenly full of disturbing sixteen-year-olds with thongs of fine plaited leather twined enticingly round their slender necks? When Rosemary had been this girl's age, she'd been firmly encased in a thick and unflattering school uniform and invariably in her narrow bed alone by ten-thirty every night of the week. Rosemary sighs at the injustice of it all, fixes the disturbing one with a beady eye, and demands a receipt for her purchase.

.

Rosemary swoops along Sid Einfeld Drive with the dead night weight of Bondi Junction a spurned, dull spouse to the right and the bright and restless view down and across the harbor tumbling away to the left. A whip of lightning flicks, though the sound of thunder closing in cannot be heard above the hum of the engine. Rosemary switches from the perpetual news hour drone of Radio National left over from the drive home that afternoon to 2JJJ and *"You, you've got the right stuff baby and I love the way you turn me on,"* which of course causes her to think about where Billie might be and what she's doing.

Round the corner and down the hill to Bondi Beach, Rosemary sees the lightning out over the sea and, winding down the window and switching off the air conditioner, she can smell the dry crackle of electricity in the air, and sense the urgent jolts of excitement communicating themselves to the crowds of cartwheeling youth on Campbell Parade.

She picks up a six-pack of Cascade lager at the Nirvana Liquor Store and cruises on to the Ploy Thai, parking in a bus zone because it is the only place to be had.

In the restaurant she eats yam pla goong, drinks her beer, and daydreams about the big blue blunt-nosed building opposite. Rosemary would like to own that building. She'd like to buy it with a group of friends and turn it into a gay and lesbian home for the elderly. The prawn salad is excellent. Rosemary has tried making it herself and the result was good, but not exact.

Something was missing. She suspects it was chili jam. She'll try that, next time.

The storm has arrived. Clouds of steam rise from the street's hot surface and the heavy summer rain floods the gutters in seconds. Rosemary stands in the doorway, watching the big drops streak down and bounce back off the pavement in bullets of pure silver. Rosemary loves the obliterating roar of it. She is, for the moment, perfectly still inside and happy. She knows she is. It is one of those moments.

.

Billie's not happy. There are two reasons for this.

The first is she's ridden far too far in one stretch, her eyes are drier and contain more grit than the Great Sandy Desert, and her eyelids are held wide apart on rusty hinges that will not close.

The second is her mother. Billie blames herself a bit for what has happened tonight. She should have allowed herself an easier trip up here so she'd arrive in a better state to deal with it, instead of all stressed-out and dusty. At first it had been the usual thing, Billie and Heather embracing, talking, catching up and happy to see each other. But it didn't take long before an edge crept in. The first thing Billie noticed about this place was that it smelled gently but nonetheless definitely of sewage. She couldn't help it. Any normal person would smell it except everyone here denied it, or else they were used to it. The slightest wrinkling of the nose put Heather instantly on the defensive and made her spout off about the polluted hellhole that was Sydney where air's not fit to breathe, streets not safe to walk along, water poisonous to drink. Billie couldn't bear to see the tight lines of disappointment that formed round her mother's eyes at these moments.

Billie wishes she could find the right words or the right actions to smooth them away, but she can't. Their relationship isn't easy. Billie still resents the way her mother always hugged other people—grungy strangers who paid to come to their house for weekend workshops, the howling participants in the appalling psychodramas that studded Billie's childhood—but never had a squeeze to spare for Billie, or if she did, it just wasn't comfortable.

Her brother Simon feels the same but he doesn't care so much, especially since he shifted to Western Australia and has a baby of his own that he carries round with him everywhere in a pouch.

The thought of Simon's baby safe inside its pouch makes Billie want to throw things and then to cry, but she doesn't want to think about all this now, trapped in a dank yurt in the middle of a paddock and needing to pee and feeling too wrecked to be bothered getting up. Billie certainly doesn't want to cry, but, after a bit of initial stinging, she realizes that the tears are making her eyes feel much better and so she continues.

While she's doing this, she reminds herself that no doubt her mother too hoped it would be different this time and that they could be relaxed together instead of, five minutes into the visit, all this barbed wire of tension winding itself round them.

Billie reminds herself of the good things about Bundagen. These include the fact that had the shareholders not bought this land when it went up for sale, it would have been parceled up and sold to developers and well and truly sunk in concrete by now, thus turning the whole east coast into one great irreversible Big Banana disaster. Then she remembers how beautiful the beach is and also you don't have to wear a bathing suit and riding a wave with nothing on feels fantastic.

What Billie doesn't understand, and possibly never will, is that what her mother wants from her has nothing to do with Billie's approval of where she has chosen to live. Heather just wants her daughter to love her and to stop being so picky about everything. She'd like to enjoy her company.

In the morning things will look different. The sun will be bright and the wind will have changed direction, taking the smell with it, and Billie will walk happily in one of her mother's bright sarongs through the small banana plantation and the mango trees and across the grassy cliff tops to the beach. The only blot on the landscape will be the local policeman and his mates bombing along the beach in their four-wheel drive screaming and yelling and carrying on in ways that Billie could well do without.

The day's major problem will be that, when she gets back around lunchtime, Crispin will have turned up. Billie and Crispin don't get on. Billie tells herself she does her best with him, although she doesn't, whereas Crispin the homophobic hippie makes no effort at all and, being American, would be astonished if anyone suggested he should.

.

"The number of melanoma cases in New South Wales has more than doubled in seven years, according to new figures."

Rosemary's woken early, but now she wishes she hadn't. Lucky she doesn't live in Queensland, though, because "the rate of deadly skin cancer in Queensland is a staggering 50 percent higher than in New South Wales."

Rosemary decides to count her blessings, stop reading the paper, and make herself a pot of Earl Grey tea, which she takes to the window where she sits and watches the day take shape.

Gail, the psychotherapist who lives in next door's top-floor flat, crosses the street with the bag of toys she uses in her sand-play therapy. And there's the fast-walking woman again. Rosemary hasn't seen her for more than a month now and supposes she's been away in a mental hospital and is making up for lost time. Gaunt, haunting, and beyond therapy, this fast-walking stick insect of a woman scrambles across the horizons of the beach suburbs of eastern Sydney from dawn to dusk and possibly all night as well for all Rosemary knows. Gail carefully sets out her toys in the sand, watched by a crowd of complacent sea gulls. The obsession of the fast-walking woman reminds Rosemary of Daphne wrapped in her gray crumbling woolens in the basement of the sociology department, though God knows

Daphne never did a minute's exercise in her life. Rosemary reminds herself of her intention to take some time this summer to get in shape. She will start today—go over to the pool and swim some laps.

She goes to her chest of drawers and pulls out her bathing suit. A cockroach comes with it. It looks a bit dazed, but dazed is not what Rosemary's paid for so she calls the pest control people, who tell her not to worry about any leftover roaches because the chemicals they used contain a special ingredient that prevents them from reaching sexual maturity and breeding. Rosemary feels she cannot argue with this, although she'd like to.

Now, where's the sunblock?

Just as she finds this and starts to apply it, the phone rings and "Good morning, Rose. It's Fiona."

Heavens! Fiona! It's been years. Fiona's been back, of course, promoting her books and visiting her mother and seeing friends but never Rosemary, so why is she calling her now?

"Because my mother's dying. I'm sitting at home with her . . . I mean I don't have to do anything, the nurses do everything for her that needs doing, it's just that, you know, she sent for me. So here I am and I'm not sure she knows I am because she's doped to the eyeballs and her mind is wandering as they say— though in her case it's not so much wandering as making up for lost time and galloping. She keeps begging anyone who'll listen—and that's everyone, of course, because everyone in this mausoleum is paid to listen—she keeps begging them to send her precious children home. Well, as we all know, I'm an only child and not a particularly precious one at that. Anyway, I was just wandering round in the garden thinking about everything and I picked up the phone book and looked you up and there you were."

"You're in Woollahra?" Rosemary immediately feels this to be a stupid question but, after all, people do move and the Woollahra house is a very large one for one woman to die in. There is the distracting thought, struggling and ashamed at the back of her mind, that she is actually, finally, glad that her own mother died early and in reasonably good order so that now Rosemary doesn't have to face the final parental disintegration increasingly witnessed by her friends.

Rosemary remembers that Cyril, Fiona's father and commonly described as a Colorful Racing Identity, is dead. She remembers reading the bit in the *Herald* about the memorial service and how all the Sydney criminals had turned up—happy to outlive him, Rosemary thought, or else just to make absolutely sure he wasn't coming back. Fiona had not come home for that death.

"Woollahra, yes. *Yes*. And very odd it is too. I mean the place is a . . . well, you'll see. When you come. You will come, won't you?"

"Yes. When?"

"Well—what about now? I take it you're not busy." A moment ago Rosemary had been pleased with her leisured state. Now she felt inadequate for not being about the world's business. Rosemary remembers Fiona's talent for undermining everyone around her. She has a good mind not to go.

•

"What the fuck is ACT UP?" inquires Crispin the retrograde creep, staring at Billie's tits through the T-shirt on which these words are written. Crispin knows what ACT UP is and Billie knows he knows but she tells him nonetheless because she has the feeling that the more you say things out loud the more they gain power even if they do mostly fall on deaf ears. She sees all this unheeded wisdom banking up on the rim of the world ready for the coming storm when these words will swoop down and sweep all the shit away. Crispin, on the other hand, sees nothing and just thinks she's mad. Crispin longs for the good old days. He'd like to arrange for a rerun of the sixties when girls knew their position in life.

Thinking of various girls he'd put in any position that pleased him, he barely hears what she's saying. AIDS Coalition to Unleash Power? Strings of initials stream past him: AZT D4T GM-CSF ddl. In his day there was no indiscretion that couldn't be put right by a shot or two of penicillin. Crispin feels old and out of it when surely it was only a minute ago he and his concerns were set squarely at the center of the world.

He can't stand these visits of Billie's; they drive him nuts. They upset her mother too. And where is Heather during all this? She's in what passes as a kitchen, considering this matter of Billie. On one hand she admires her. Heather knows it is important to tackle attitudes. It might be like boxing a mist but it's a bout that has to be fought. On the other hand, her daughter's judgmental ways are not admirable, and when it comes to herself, they are badly mistaken. Billie knows next to nothing of Heather's life in this community and yet she feels free to mock it. Heather does not feel compelled to explain herself to Billie, but her daughter's scorn is hurtful. Take, for example, this place. Billie might despise it but this yurt is hers and it is not so easy for a girl to own any part of this world. She listens as Billie defends the concept of "outing" to an accompaniment of strangled protest from Crispin. What an arrogant young woman her Billie has turned out to be. The world is not as simple as it might look to a girl who is headed for the thirty-seventh floor of somewhere whether she thinks she is or not. But she'll learn, thinks Heather, as has many a mum before her. Heather regrets that some of these lessons she knows Billie must learn will be hard. Heather has always been saddened by the harshness of the world while Billie seems to thrive on it, bouncing about and creating strife wherever she goes. The list of things she's taken up against since she first drew breath is endless. Take men, for example.

"You take them," yelps Billie, bursting into the kitchen and out again to get some fresh air, though first she must disentangle herself from the seashells strung on strings in the place where, in any proper house, you might expect to find a door. Billie vows that she will never live in any house that doesn't have a decent door to slam.

Heather, making a mango lassi as solace for Crispin who's sulking in the corner and threatening to move back out to

Nimbin, wonders why Billie gets so worked up over someone like Crispin. He is, after all, just one member of the tribe of lost boys who inhabit our part of the earth, to be kept calm and placated occasionally but never, surely, to be taken as seriously as Billie takes them. Heather is fond of Crispin, but she keeps him in perspective. Heather hands Crispin his lassi and Crispin hands her back a grudging smile. Crispin often feels the urge to escape but he's taking herbs for it.

Heather looks at the photograph her son Simon enclosed in his Christmas letter, which is pinned to the cork notice board above the bench. Simon, his wife Patrice, and baby Jake. Heather smiles. Simon's so simple, compared with his sister. Is this a joke? No, it's true.

Billie—for whom nothing is simple and never will be, she hopes—lopes through the scrub eager to remind herself exactly who she is and what world it is she belongs in and so she needs to find the public phone that she is sure is hidden behind a tree somewhere round here. Billie realizes, as she blunders about in the bush trying to make a connection, that what she needs is a mobile phone. She finds the phone booth and puts through a collect call to Rosemary, but it doesn't get her anywhere because Rosemary is out and the operator won't let Billie leave a message on the machine for nothing. So she tries JoJo in Glebe and sundry others, but they're all out too.

·

*R*osemary gets out of her car in front of the crumbling mansion called Lullsworth. Why it was called this she has no idea.

She notes the arsenic highlights and umber wastes of its crumbling facade. The garden scrunches and drips around her, all snails and plumbago. Weeds are storming up the steps to the front door. A spindly old dog wobbles over to greet her. It seems pleased to see Rosemary, its three yellow teeth sliding sideways as it slobbers on her shoe.

There used to be a tennis court here somewhere. There it is. It's behind the house, a big bowl of weeds with a vast dust-cover of morning glory flung across it.

"Piss off, Deborah . . ." Fiona bursts out of the front door and sends the dog staggering away. "You're a brute. Last of a long line of Mother's vile brutes. It'll be off to the vet with you one of these fine mornings, you just see if it won't," and to Rosemary: "You remember all those fleabags of Mother's, don't you?"

Rosemary isn't sure she does. What she does remember is how Fiona has always become worked up over everything equally, so that the smallest thing arouses as much passion as the largest. It was impressive and it was exhausting. Fiona is tall, gaunt, and gray, her limbs arranged at dramatic angles. Rosemary thinks she is just like she used to be only more so. Fiona's alarming green eyes examine Rosemary, who feels as though she's being pinned against her car and thoroughly frisked for hidden weapons.

"How are you?" she asks.

"How should I be?" asks Fiona, who doesn't know and why should she?

What words are there for age's evils; the ruck and the wrinkle, the hoar-hair, the drooping, the dying, the winding sheets, the tombs and worms, and the final tumbling to decay? How are you supposed to be in the face of all that? Besides, Fiona and her mother have never got on.

Fiona takes Rosemary's arm and walks her firmly up the steps and through the front door, which shuts behind them and falls off its hinges with a bang. Fiona starts to laugh and, once she realizes she hasn't been hurt, so does Rosemary.

"Honestly," gasps Fiona, "talk about the fall of the House of Usher. It is, isn't it? Exactly like that?"

It is, thinks Rosemary, and nods her agreement because laughing so hard has left her with a stitch. Rosemary folds herself up on the bottom step of the grand staircase that rears up behind her until lost in shadow, and struggles to get her breath back.

Above her head two sensible shoes descend out of the gloom and into the light to be followed by two thick but endearing ankles.

"It's lunchtime," announces a voice from the realm of darkness. "And your ma's feeling lively."

"Okay, Bridget, thanks."

"I'll be back by half past one at the latest," says this Bridget, and as she completes her descent of the stairs Rosemary's head finds itself intimately enveloped in strange skirts, which is not unpleasant. Bridget leaves without so much as a look or a comment concerning the state of the front door. Perhaps her mind's on lunch or perhaps she's seen it all before.

"They're always Irish, you know," says Fiona. "All these

nurses and social workers and physiotherapists and what have you, they always are. They're marvelous. This one is, anyway. Mother's quite attached to her, it seems. At least she behaves better when Bridget's around. Well, we'd best go up and see what's going on."

Mother lies alone, as she's done for years, and despite what they've been told she appears to be asleep with a light cotton blanket bundled up under her sharp chin. Or is she unconscious, wonders Rosemary, at a loss to tell the difference. There's this worrying wisp of dull orange hair that's fallen across her face and rises and falls at each breath. Rosemary waits for Fiona to lift it away, but Fiona appears reluctant to do anything, so Rosemary does. The old woman's eyes snap open.

"Why is a Filofax like a clitoris?"

Rosemary cannot begin to think. Perhaps Fiona knows but Fiona's over by the window with her back turned.

"I don't know."

"You'd better ask me then."

"Why is it?"

"Why is what?"

Fiona is struggling to open the window. She smacks and bangs at several generations of paint.

"Why is a Filofax like a clitoris?"

"She won't rest until she's torn the place down round my ears. Look at her, she's mad. My mad daughter. She kicked in the front door a minute ago. I heard her." The old woman has slipped down on her pillows. She tries and fails to raise herself.

Rosemary does her best to straighten her out but she is nervous and clumsy and the blanket slides to the floor, revealing an unexpected nakedness. Rosemary restores the blanket. She wants to say something but she cannot remember her name. Mrs. Henty, yes, but what was her name? Lillian, was that it? Rosemary's fairly sure it was something beginning with L. This lack of a name seems particularly absurd. Rosemary's eyes fill with tears. The old woman sees this and smiles. It is quite a kind smile and it reminds Rosemary of the old dog.

"I remember you," the old woman tells her. "Yes. You're the serious one who used to moon about after her highness. Not that it would've done you much good. You wouldn't get far with old iron bloomers over there. You're a teacher now, aren't you?"

Rosemary nods. She supposes this is more or less what she is.

"Thought so. You were the type. I did nothing all my life. Never felt the need. I had money. Nothing struck me as so important you'd want to spend your life doing it, day in and day out. Real estate was my passion."

Fiona turns now, is watching her mother and her friend arranged in what she considers to be a rather shabby Dickensian tableau. "Not like some who think they can change the world with their rantings. 'Life is real, life is earnest, and the grave is not the goal,' " quotes the woman in a fair imitation of her daughter at her worst.

Fiona picks up the phone by the bed and calls someone to come and block off the front door. "No," she says, "it doesn't have to be that elaborate. You can just board it up and make it secure. Nobody's going to be going in or out."

"She's going to have me taken out through the kitchen. She's been after me for years to sell this place and move somewhere sensible as she calls it, but I always told her, 'No, you'll have to take me out of here in a box.' Didn't think I'd be leaving through the back door though. Not the grand exit I imagined. That'll please her. That's why she kicked the door down, of course."

"She didn't break it. It was an accident. It fell apart. It was old, I expect."

Rosemary starts to feel foolish, like a child again, out of her depth but compelled to stick up for her friend. Then, as now, she does not expect to be believed. It doesn't sound very likely, does it? But why the hell doesn't Fiona say something?

"I used to beat her regularly, you know. But instead of beating the badness out of her, I only succeeded in beating it further in."

Fiona and her mother look at each other. Rosemary senses the spark of malicious complicity that crackles between them and feels excluded. Dreadful childhood games of blindman's bluff come to mind, with her the plodding, bamboozled, blinded one in the middle. What's she doing here, anyway? She and Fiona weren't close, not at school they weren't and not afterward either, with Fiona already beady-eyed with ambition, and then she'd gone to England and that had been that.

Rosemary had gone overseas too, and lived in London for

some years untouched by Fiona's rising illustriousness. They had lived within two streets of each other in W10 even as Fiona wrote and Rosemary, in time, read that brilliant book, but that was another story.

Rosemary thinks of that other story now as she sits caught in the cross fire. Or is it a fragment of a thought really? A sliver of the story as a door opens, and there in it stands the woman but you do not look up, you keep on working in your place at the table piled high with books and papers because you do not want her to speak and because her name is Miriam and not Sapphire, the one you want. Miriam has a purple and gray scarf, a pale lavender twin set. She can be undressed. How long is it since anyone wore that sort of bra? You'd forgotten about the Band-Aid-colored underwear but you remember it now better than you remember the body beneath it that in itself is an exaggeration of breasts and pubic hair done in black and white as this final picture elbows its way up from the darkness and leaves you here, now, today, sitting in this bedroom where you shake your head because you do not want this old sharp bit of story lodged in it. You want to stay as large as the years have made you. And still there is that look that stretches like a trip wire between two women. Fiona and Lillian. Rosemary thinks the woman's name must be Lillian. There aren't that many names that begin with L. She's been through them all and Lillian seems right.

"She hates me. She's quite right to."

Rosemary looks at Fiona. Come on, Fiona, say something, please. Fiona tells her mother not to be silly.

"Silly? I may have been worldly and venal, my girl, but thank God I've never been silly."

Then there is this long silence and Rosemary notices that it is twelve noon by the bedside clock, which must be slow, and that Lillian's gaze has slipped, turned itself away toward some inner thing. Fiona's hand reaches for one of the disposable syringes that are heaped in a stainless steel kidney-shaped dish on the chest of drawers and Rosemary finds herself out on the landing. Dust, sweet and mothy, rises from the stringy remains of the Tabriz runner under her feet. She's always been hopeless when it comes to needles.

The angel of the Lord brought the tidings to Mary.

Inside the room Fiona takes a vial of clear liquid from a square leather case in which many such are nestled, breaks the seal,

And she conceived by the Holy Ghost.

pierces the top with the needle, fills the syringe and

Hail Mary, full of Grace, the Lord

injects her mother smoothly in the left buttock with whatever it is, and

is with thee, blessed art thou . . .

drops the syringe into the wastepaper basket.

"I've been practicing giving injections to grapefruit," says Fiona, joining Rosemary on the landing. It used to be that when Rosemary recited the *Angelus* the phrases had gone on in her head no matter what the interruption, but that was a long time ago and now they did not.

Lillian is definitely asleep now. Fiona thinks they should go and get themselves something to eat. She leads Rosemary downstairs and to the kitchen through moldering rooms in which most of the furniture is turning green. Rosemary's spirits dip further but then, happily, the kitchen is in reasonable shape and sunny and contains several delicious things from David Jones's gourmet food shop.

Rosemary scoops up a spoonful of salmon roe and eats it. She adores these perfect orange pearls that taste like Billie. But where is Billie? And what is Rosemary to make of today and why had Fiona asked her here? Rosemary decides that Fiona needed some company, someone to talk to for a while, but that she has an image to preserve. These scenes, the rotting house, are not things she can expose to anyone she considers important and so she'd phoned Rosemary. Rosemary can't know this for sure, but that's her guess. Meanwhile, Fiona's taking a silver cocktail shaker out of the fridge.

"Did you really fancy me when we were children?"

Rosemary isn't quite sure what she's talking about, then remembers Lillian saying something like that up in the bedroom. She'd fancied a few girls at school, especially those like Fiona, older and bolder than she, so she has to think for a second.

"No. I didn't."

"Do you now?"

Rosemary shakes her head. She decides to overlook this nonsense on the grounds that Fiona's mother is dying upstairs, but Fiona, it seems, really wants to talk about this.

"That's a shame. I gave up on men years ago. They're all

emotional two-year-olds. I wish I was lesbian. I mean, I like women more than I like men but . . . well, I've tried it, you know . . . in bed, and it just doesn't work for me. I wish it did."

Rosemary treats herself to another scoop of salmon roe. She wonders what would have happened if she'd said she did fancy Fiona. Would Fiona have tried to give the girls another try? Would she have led Rosemary to a mildewed bed in the east wing? Rosemary can understand this. A good fuck can be very consoling.

Fiona pours two drinks and pushes one across the table. Rosemary presses a few fizzy eggs against her front teeth with her tongue.

"Cheers," says Fiona. They drink. The drink proves to be a martini, which is always a welcome diversion. But Fiona will not be diverted.

"Even when I used to have affairs with married men, I always ended up liking their wives much more than I ever liked them."

Rosemary sniffs her drink. The crisp cleansing smell of it cuts through the traces of death and dust and mold that have been dawdling about in her nose. She resists the impulse to dab a drop of it behind each ear. When she dies, can she be lowered into a large glass tube of this pleasing mix and hang suspended, a big cool olive facing eternity?

"I was a miserable child."

Rosemary's not surprised. She thinks of the old woman dying

upstairs. She thinks of the decaying house, the festering garden. She thinks a bulldozer might be a good idea. She would like to change the subject and opens her mouth to do so but she's too late.

"My father was not my father. She said he was and I thought he was. I don't know what he thought. I mean, I know he knew he wasn't. He's covered a lot of tracks."

"Who is he then? I mean . . . who is your father?"

"Who was my father, you mean. He's dead. And I can't tell you who he was. Not yet. I never would have found out but then, one morning, I came across this piece of paper in the British Museum."

"Heavens," says Rosemary, for want of anything better.

"You can imagine the shock."

"Yes," says Rosemary, though what she actually imagines is this unlikely piece of paper floating about in the British Museum waiting for Fiona to pluck it out of the air and discover the truth about her ancestry.

"But your mother must know, surely?"

Fiona thumps the table. The martinis dance. "She won't say. She says it's none of my business. She says I'm making it up because there's a book in it somewhere. But I'm not making it up. And there *is* a book in it somewhere. I intend to find it."

Rosemary thinks she can hear the dry trembling of old bones in the treetops; it comes from the place where all the dear dead fathers go to ground.

Banging from the front of the house indicates that someone

has come to seal off the door. Fiona goes to supervise. Rosemary finishes the salmon roe and decides to leave. First she goes upstairs to say good-bye to Lillian.

She knocks on the door, which opens promptly. Bridget's head appears round it. Farts and fizzing noises streak past her ears and sink into the bottomless dark of the stairwell.

"Oh dear," says Bridget, "we're in the most terrible uproar this afternoon, and not up to visitors at all, I'm afraid."

Rosemary goes downstairs and looks for Fiona. The workman thinks she's gone for a walk with the dog. Rosemary goes to her car, gets in. She starts the engine. Should she go without saying good-bye? She does. As she pulls out of the driveway, she sees Fiona and the dog walking down the street. Rosemary slows and stops beside them. Fiona instructs the dog to sit and comes round to the driver's side of the car. Rosemary winds down the window.

"Thanks for coming," says Fiona.

"I'm sorry about your mother," says Rosemary, who would like to say more but knows that Fiona will not let her. "If there's anything I can do . . . ?" But there isn't. Rosemary pats Fiona's hand, which rests on the window frame. Fiona smiles and withdraws it.

Rosemary drives away. Fiona and the lopsided dog diminish in the rearview mirror and vanish into the shadowy afternoon. Too late Rosemary realizes that she still does not know why a Filofax is like a clitoris.

•

*T*here's no message on the machine from Billie. What there is, though, is a request for a lift up to this commitment ceremony on Saturday from a woman Rosemary doesn't know. Rosemary isn't pleased. Who is she, who gave her Rosemary's name and number, and why can't she catch the train?

Next comes an indecipherable mumble from Daphne, sounding as though she needs a blood transfusion. What she says sounds like "send lawyers, guns, and money" but that couldn't possibly be right and—this was better—a clear, crisp call from Alan suggesting a movie and dinner tonight. Good. Rosemary can't wait to tell someone about Fiona, and Alan will do nicely, though she'll have to sit through a film before she gets her chance. While denying that he likes gossip, Alan does admit to an interest in detail. Rosemary phones him at his office in Juniper Hall and they agree to meet at the Academy Twin for the seven o'clock session and eat afterward.

She thinks about Daphne. She should phone back. Daphne hardly ever telephones anyone so it must be important. But on the other hand does she feel like dealing with whatever it is at this moment? Probably not. She'll call first thing tomorrow. No, she won't. She'll call now, or else she'll feel guilty all night. Rosemary dials Daphne's direct number at the university. No answer. Rosemary looks up Daphne's home number in her address book. Daphne lives in Lilyfield, in a housing department flat. No answer there either, but at least she'd tried.

Rosemary picks up the *Spectator* she bought at the newsagent on the way home and goes out into her small garden to read it. Kristeva accompanies her to shorten some lizards.

She wishes Billie would call.

.

The motorbike goes into the corner low and tight. When they hit the straight Crispin raises his arms, flings back his head, and hollers. Billie laughs, screws up her eyes in the face of the sun hanging low in front of her as the road turns from the coast, and takes them west.

They are on their way to Nimbin, where Crispin has his wasabi patch. Billie wants to see it. Crispin just wants a ride on her Harley so it suits him, though he does wish she'd let him drive. Maybe she will on the way back but then again maybe she won't. If their positions were reversed he's sure he wouldn't let her drive it, but girls are much nicer so he reckons if he chooses his moment and asks her really nicely he's got a chance.

Billie's planning to leave tomorrow. Right now she's admiring Crispin's wasabi patch, which is indeed admirable. Some years back Crispin, having observed the growing popularity of Japanese food in Australia and the fact that the wasabi that went with it was invariably imported, started growing it himself. His idea had worked. He supplies the best Japanese restaurants with fresh and flawless wasabi and now he plans to expand. He's put out feelers. Now, it seems, Crispin is on the verge of exporting his wasabi to Japan, which pleases him very much. Something of his enthusiasm touches Billie as he stands beside her outlining his next project, which is bonsai vegetables.

Billie looks at Crispin. He is a small thin man. With a silver earring and a navy workshirt tucked into soft moleskin trousers held up by one of those plaited belts, he looks good. Billie smiles at him. Without thinking about it, Crispin smiles back at the person he glimpses behind the irritating ACT UP T-shirt.

The setting sun leaves a glow behind the rain-forested hills that encircle this place. Crispin watches.

"Have you ever seen *le rai en vert*?"

"No."

She hasn't heard of it either. What is it? He tells her that it is green rays of light that on rare occasions flare up from beneath the horizon just after the sun has set. Anyone who witnesses this phenomenon can expect great good luck; he's been looking all his life and never seen it.

"Well, you have now," says Billie, nodding at the horizon. And she's right. There it is.

"But I've been looking for years," cries Crispin, who, despite his advanced age, is sometimes stung by the universe and its unjust ways.

"Beginner's luck," shrugs Billie.

Yeah. Well. He has to admit that luck is luck no matter who has it. He's fortunate to find himself in its fleeting presence. Crispin bounces back. His wasabi patch and future bonsai vegetables are bound to be successful.

"I don't believe in luck," says Billie.

"Well, you should," he tells her.

"Wanna drive?" she asks, tossing him the keys.

.

Daphne sits at her desk tapping the cardboard binder of the top notebook of a pile of ten notebooks with a long, varnished fingernail, chipped. The notebooks are all the same, all handsome, all made in France before the Second World War. This pile is one of ten piles of notebooks on her desk, ten piles containing ten years of Ethel Daintree's jottings, which makes one hundred notebooks all identical and all in an impenetrable shorthand that had been used for a minute in New Zealand—impenetrable at least until this morning, when a dictionary had arrived at her door, sent by an old man in Arkansas, an authority on early forms of shorthand who had a special fondness for the baroque, complicated, and consequently unpopular form in which Daphne's quarry had chosen to keep her diaries. Daphne had tracked this fellow down via her American agent and now she has the key to all this painstakingly mysterious text safe in her smoky dungeon in Sydney.

This is a big moment. She savors it. She sighs, lights a cigarette, considers her chipped nail polish, sighs again. Wonders whether it's worth starting to transcribe the notebooks tonight. She feels excited, certain that light is at last going to be shed on the story of her mother, the writer Isobel McGuinness. She is anxious to begin, but, at the same time, she's nervous. Isobel's in the air tonight all right. Daphne can almost feel her cold dead breath on her neck. This haunting habit is one reason Daphne is so keen to confine Isobel to the pages of a book that could then be closed and placed on a shelf, out of sight and out of mind. Another is the desire to bring her neglected parent the recognition she so badly wanted and indeed deserved during her lifetime.

Ethel Daintree had been Isobel's oldest and closest friend. There had been some talk of an affair at the time, leading to Ethel's long exile overseas in the years covered by the diaries.

Daphne reaches for her own notebook and writes down these and some other thoughts, which have to do with the practical allocation of the limited monies she has received from the Literature Board for what she is doing. She writes it down in plain English because not only has she nothing to hide, it's also part of the process.

She tries calling Rosie again. This time there is no answer and no answering machine either; clearly Rosemary has gone out gallivanting and forgotten to leave it on.

Daphne switches on her desk lamp, lights a cigarette, and inhales deeply, dragging the smoke as far down into her lungs as she can so it scratches, reminding her in a comforting way that she does exist. She could give herself a good pinch too, and sometimes she does.

She finds her bottle of scotch, fails to find a clean glass and so, unless she wants to walk along the corridor to the toilets to rinse it out, which she doesn't, must use the one she used this morning and indeed last night and probably yesterday morning as well. Daphne tips the scotch into the smeary glass and, thus armed, opens the cardboard cover and turns the first page of the first diary.

.

Alan has never liked these very British costume dramas but Rosemary enjoys them and so, until now, he's sat through them for her sake. Tonight he can't summon the state of derisive boredom he often conjures up to keep himself amused. The same could be said of his life. Alan occasionally sees that he has become less tolerant of everything. His friends see this and talk about it when he isn't there. In fact, Rosemary intends to try and talk to him about his growing tetchiness with the world later on. Over dinner if she feels she can. It worries her to see her friend getting so set in his ways and closed to everything new. Is it to do with aging, this intellectual hardening of the arteries, and will it happen to her, she asks herself as they settle in at the restaurant.

It's not the place she would have chosen but, having had her way with the film, she's decided to give way on the question of where they would eat. When they are seated at another table, Alan, having insisted on moving from the one reserved for them because it's too close to a speaker spewing musical glue— Rosemary has to say, in this case, he is absolutely right—he picks up his glass.

"We had a threesome last night," he says, raising the glass in salute. "Cheers."

Rosemary knows who "we" are.

"I thought you'd—you know—agreed to stop all that."

"Well, I had. I have, really. I don't think it'll happen again. But last night they came over for dinner and afterward Kurt got very—well, Kurt wanted it, so what was Tristram going to do—I mean he's not going to storm out and leave me and Kurt to it, is he?" Alan laughs.

"Well, cheers then." Rosemary drinks to Alan's threesome because he seems so pleased with it.

"I mean," adds Alan, by way of a postscript, "it doesn't worry me, but I bet they were up all night fighting. So it probably won't happen again."

"You sound a bit wistful."

"Wistful? Don't think so. No. How's young Billie getting on?"

"All right, I expect."

They set about the business of ordering, which Rosemary finds difficult because her eyesight has suddenly packed up, though matters improve when she holds the menu at arm's length. Alan takes off his glasses and hands them to her.

"Better?"

"Yes."

"Thought so. Happened to me about six months ago. Bingo. Right on target, the ophthalmologist said. It happens when you're our age."

It's not appropriate to scream in a crowded restaurant just because you've glimpsed the lid of the world closing on you like a coffin, so Rosemary doesn't. Instead she makes her choices and hands the glasses back to Alan.

"I hated the film."

"I know you did." They have already gone through this on the way here. "I found it quite entertaining. Restful. You know."

"No. I don't know. I hate that taxidermist school of film-making. I don't mind watching it on television so much. At least then you can get on with your ironing."

"Sorry. Next time, you choose."

"I will."

Their eyes lock in a mutual glare. Surprised, both look away and are saved by the approach of the waiter. Both feel they'd better watch out. Friends are important. Speaking of which, Rosemary still hasn't been in touch with Sara and Susan. She'll phone them tomorrow.

This was one of those violently noisy Sydney restaurants with too many hard edges. A knife or fork touching china sounded like cannon fire.

"Well," says Alan, casting a critical eye over the plate of antipasto crashing down between them, "and what've you been up to?" Rosemary spears a sun-dried tomato and, in view of her own tetchiness, shelves her plans to tackle Alan about his and tells him about Fiona, instead.

·

*N*ext morning Alan faxes her a copy of the death notice from the *Sydney Morning Herald.* Lillian had died late yesterday afternoon while her daughter was taking the dog for a walk. Rosemary phones the house in Woollahra. Busy, busy, and then no answer. Kristeva sits singing on the kitchen counter. Rosemary scoops her up and walks to the window. Poor Fiona.

There's a short fat body lying washed up on the sand at the northern end of the beach. A police car careens down the hill past the jeering group of boys playing the Street Fighter game outside the laundromat. The boys take off after it through the park, leaving the horrible game to bark, blip, and scream to itself. The police car stops outside the surf club. Two policemen get out and lumber across the sand. The boys dance around them. Rosemary drops Kristeva, leaps to her telescope, and applies her eye.

The circular world of the telescope, startling in its detail, collides with a rubbish bin in the park, lurches into a tree, and veers past the DANGEROUS RIP sign before flipping out to sea to rebound off a Russian container ship stuck on the horizon and cutting a swath through the surfers off Tamarama. Then it turns for home, where it lands on the smooth, spotted slope of the belly of a leopard seal. Rosemary fiddles with the focus, pulls back to see the whole picture as the police cordon off the area and people hurry across the park. Rosemary runs out to join them.

A drab van enters the park and, ignoring the concrete vehicle access road, churns toward them across the grass. This van has a bemused looking panda painted on its side.

"I'm from ORCA," announces the driver of the van, a somber creature in a compost-colored uniform.

"What planet's that?" inquires Theresa, who lives in the flat next to the fish and chip shop. This establishment's ventilator fan blows into Theresa's bedroom and she often smells like an old chip. A strange thing is, Theresa often has bits of glitter sticking to her face. They're there now.

"G'day, trooper," cries Theresa, as she spots Rosemary standing beside her. She slaps Rosemary on the shoulder, as is her way.

Rosemary and Theresa used to go snorkeling together early in the morning, pursuing fleeting fish through the submerged graveyard of shopping trolleys beyond the rocks at the southern end of the beach. Clambering out over the rocks on one particularly glittery morning when Theresa's face sparkled like a Christmas tree, Rosemary had reached out to touch it but ended up touching one of Theresa's large breasts. She'd done it without thinking, without meaning to, as far as she knew. Theresa had stepped back looking closed and cautious. Rosemary had stepped over some line she shouldn't have and, worse, couldn't work out why she'd done it. She'd felt ashamed; a sexual harasser, a queer Queer.

Seconds later Rosemary, distracted by her foolishness, had slipped and, rather than risk further offense, she'd chosen not to reach out and grab Theresa to regain her balance. Instead she had fallen and scraped the backs of her legs, cutting her right elbow on the sharp bits of shells that bristled on the rocks. Blood flowed. Theresa had hauled the distressed Rosemary to her feet and, placing a firm arm round her waist, assisted her back to the beach. Once there, Theresa had mopped at the blood with her towel and declared the wounds to be just a few scratches and nothing to worry about. Rosemary was glad to hear it, though she worried about infection. After all, no one in their right minds would eat the shellfish that grew out there, so surely if they cut you who knew what toxins would flow instantly into your bloodstream?

"You'll be all right, trooper," said Theresa, who was clearly intending to abandon Rosemary and stomp back out over the rocks to retrieve her gear and resume her morning's plan.

"Thanks," said Rosemary.

"No more funny business then, eh?" said Theresa. Despite the rising intonation, this was by no means intended as a question. Bruised and foolish, Rosemary nodded. Theresa nodded back and set off toward the water. Before she'd vanished into the morning dazzle she'd turned and given Rosemary the thumbs-up sign, which she'd taken to be a gesture of forgiveness. Rosemary's arm had started to ache. She'd limped home where she was sure she had a jar of pawpaw ointment left over from the time she'd fallen off her bike in Centennial Park. She'd rub it on and bring out the bruise.

"I bet it's sick," says Theresa, back in the present once the past has passed and they're watching this ORCA person slip under the barrier and crawl toward the seal, talking into a portable phone as he goes. "Or if it isn't sick now, it soon will be."

"It's a girl," says one of the cops, sagely.

"How would he know?" growls Theresa, but Rosemary sees

the soft sweet curve of belly and thinks it must be. "What do you reckon, mate?" roars Theresa at the ORCA person, who's obviously not willing to share any of his expertise as he whips a steel tape measure out of his pocket and proceeds to measure the sleepy seal, reporting his findings to whoever listens at the end of the phone.

The seal sneezes and rolls over with a great air-wrenching gasp, releasing a dark sardiney smell and pinning the bloke from ORCA beneath her. The little boys laugh and so do Rosemary and Theresa as the police rush forward and roll the seal off. The man from ORCA rises and brushes himself off. He looks suspiciously at his phone before banging it sharply on the heel of his shoe. He presses its gritty buttons, holds it to his ear, grimaces in disgust, and trudges back over the sand to his panda van. The seal rolls onto its back and flaps its flippers in the air. The gesture raises a ragged cheer. Somehow the growing crowd is siding with the seal against its benefactor.

Storm and his twin sister Skye, who run the surf shop, trot across the sand. Skye has her camera. She slips under the tape and walks quietly toward the seal.

"Poor girl," she croons. "Poor tired girl."

"Oh, well. She'd know," says Theresa.

"Oi! Come back. You can't do that," yells the man from ORCA. He carries a new phone, a bucket, and a length of rope.

Storm asks why not, but the man from ORCA isn't telling. Skye kneels beside the seal and pats its head. The seal snuffles. The crowd sighs; it's as though their collective breath can soothe and save the seal, raise her up and out over the sea, return her to the soft gray waves. Smooth, seal-shaped clouds form above their heads.

The police, big bums grinding, guns bumping on their hips, toil back across the park to get hamburgers and thick shakes from the Lebanese takeout. The seal clouds jostle. The crowd too jostles, closing ranks against the man from ORCA. It's going to rain. Skye starts taking photographs.

"Hey, you can't do that."

"Why can't she do that, mate?" Storm asks again, on a rising note of fury.

"She's disturbing it."

"How's she doing that then, eh?"

"Whose seal is it, anyway?" someone wants to know.

Lightning divides the world in half. Is this an answer of some kind? Thunder rumbles round the rim of the park. Another vehicle is crossing the grass toward them.

"You just want us all to go away," accuses Storm. "So's you can come back down here after dark and make love to it."

The man from ORCA thinks he's never come across such a pack of mad people in his life. He doesn't have to worry; reinforcements have arrived. The zoo truck pulls up with a car containing a news crew close behind.

"Jeez. Must be a slow news day," says Theresa.

The storm mumbles on at a distance. A few flat raindrops fall and then forget. Hope of divine intervention fades. A stretcher is unloaded and rushed across the sand to the seal. The man from ORCA fills his bucket and dashes ocean in the seal's face. He stands back, holding the rope. The seal rears up, its mouth open to release a tired roar. The man from ORCA lassoes it and runs backward, pulling the rope tight, toppling the seal, which is rolled onto the stretcher. A tarpaulin is placed over it and the man from ORCA gets busy with his rope again. When the seal is thoroughly parceled they heave it to shoulder height and jog smartly up the beach toward the truck, knees high and sprightly and heads with bright smiles turned toward the cameraman running along beside. At the cameraman's request, they do it all again. As they rush past Rosemary the second time, she sees the seal's eyes, hot and dry with a film of fear across them.

Storm pursues them up the beach, interposes his head between the seal and the camera to ask why they can't leave the seal alone to sleep and make its own way back out to sea. The zoo people say that the seal is probably suffering from a viral infection and only they can save it. Also, they want to put a tag on the seal and track it for the rest of its life. Storm grabs the man from ORCA and asks him how a slime-green eco-fascist like him would feel if some bloody great seal stuck a tag on his earhole. Rosemary thinks Storm has a point. She decides to write a letter to the *Herald* about it.

"It is better this way," insists an elderly Greek woman. "These men, they know best."

"These men know fuck-all," says Theresa.

"They'll let it go when it's better," the girl who does the ironing at the laundromat tells her.

"Why they do that? A seal is a valuable thing. You can make a beautiful coat with it."

The seal is lashed onto the back of the truck. The aptly named Storm flings his arms round it in a final embrace before turning away and stalking along the beach accompanied by his twin and by his dog, a white bullterrier that has a black leather collar studded with rhinestones, and the ugliest balls Rosemary has ever seen on any living creature. Rosemary has read that white dogs with pink noses who live at the beach run a very high risk of skin cancer. She resists the urge to worry that funny patch on her lip with her tongue. Rosemary doesn't want to see cancer at every turn, but she can't help it. Perhaps the seal has cancer. Perhaps cancer is destined to take over as an alternative form of life.

The zoo truck departs. The news team packs up and goes. The man from ORCA picks up his bucket, makes one last phone call, and follows suit. All that remains is the expanse of seal-flattened sand and the police tape fluttering in the wind. There is nothing for the crowd to do but disperse, though some ghost of the drama lingers and makes them uneager to do so.

"Well, troopers," says Theresa, taking them all in hand, "I reckon we should call the zoo every day to see how it's getting on. That'd be the right thing to do, wouldn't it?"

"I agree," agrees the girl who does the ironing at the laundromat.

Theresa and Rosemary wander along the sand toward the rock pool. Two boys are in a tug-of-war with a wet suit.

"I said you could wear it last time," says the owner, as it stretches like gaudy chewing gum between them, "but you do farts in it."

The accused one collapses with laughter, letting the wet suit go. Released, the suit springs at its owner, slapping him firmly to the ground. "Farts in my wettie," he sings, choking with laughter, "farts in my wettie."

Rosemary wonders, much as she did when she was five or six or seven and will still wonder at sixty-five or -six or -seven and will do so at a hundred and five if it proves necessary, just what exactly *is* the point of boys. It would be nice, though, to laugh so much over nothing.

"How's it going then?" Theresa nudges Rosemary with her hip. "How's your little mate getting on up north? Heard from her yet, have you?"

Rosemary tells Theresa Billie hasn't phoned, which elicits such a pitying look she immediately wishes she'd lied.

"She'll ring when she can."

"I'm sure she will," croons Theresa, in what Rosemary suspects is intended as a comforting tone. "What's that on your lip then, darling? Cold sore, is it?"

"Yes." Yes, of course it is. A cold sore and that's all. Cured, light-headed, Rosemary touches Theresa's arm. Theresa steps away and says, "Don't."

"Don't what?"

"Touch me. Don't do that."

"Well, I didn't mean . . . I mean, I didn't . . . listen, Theresa,

I'm sorry about that day. I didn't mean to upset you." Theresa's crying. What does this mean? What can it mean? "I'm sorry. The thing is, you've just done me a very good turn. I thought I had cancer and I don't. It's only a cold sore after all."

"I wouldn't count on it. I'm not a doctor."

"No. You're right though, I'm sure. I've been really neurotic lately. It's just that Billie's so much younger than I am and . . ."—should she be confiding these things to Theresa?—"it's made me very conscious of getting old."

"It would. I can see that. I don't think that's so neurotic. It seems like a normal response to me. It's what you'd expect." Theresa the understanding, Theresa the wise. Why's she crying?

"What's the matter?" Rosemary would like to put an arm round her, but she doesn't dare.

Theresa walks away. "I'm going home," she says, and goes.

•

*R*osemary enters the passage beside the fish and chips shop and skirts the big tin drums of vegetable oil piled there. One slip and she'd be pinned beneath them undiscovered for days, with cockroaches making nests in her eyes. Theresa's door stands ajar. Inside the flat, greasy curtains swath the windows. It's dark, creepy even, and what's more, Rosemary finds she's not alone. There's a crowd of people in here, standing still and silent. As her eyes adjust Rosemary finds herself in the company of saints.

Rosemary recognizes Saints Martha, Rita, Theresa, Catherine, and Clare of Assisi. Off in the corner lurks Saint Rose of Lima, her face, bearing the vicious flush of her skin disease, mercifully turned to the wall. But where's Our Lady? Rosemary should have guessed; Our Lady's in the bedroom with Theresa, who's on her bed, wrapped in a blanket, rocking herself back and forth, curled round some secret wound. There's an odd smell in this room, not immediately related to fish and chips.

Rosemary sits beside Theresa on what proves to be a futon. Rosemary considers futons a joke; they must be, mustn't they? Rosemary's noticed the people who have them take them seriously but she's not changing her mind. She reaches out and pats Theresa's heaving shoulder. Theresa erupts like a boil in the bed.

"What?"

"I don't know what. You tell me." Rosemary's getting cross. Her life is suddenly full of unreasonable, miserable people: Daphne, Alan, Fiona, and now Theresa. Middle age, thinks Rosemary. Gravity wins. It drags you down, so look out.

She looks to Our Lady for guidance but she's not much help, which comes as no surprise to Rosemary.

"I never asked you to come in, so go away."

"Well, if you're sure. You know where I am if you need me," adds Rosemary, wondering why she feels compelled to state the obvious. She should do something. She remembers there's a brother.

"Is there anyone you'd like me to phone for you? Perhaps your brother? To tell them you're not well?"

Theresa leaps from her bed, throws a punch, misses, and then seems disinclined to go on with it, which is lucky because Rosemary isn't used to this sort of thing and wouldn't have a clue how to defend herself.

Where's Billie? Billie could sort this out. Once, walking on Balmoral Beach, she'd been forced to straighten out a gang of homophobic Scots boys.

"Faggot," the biggest and most determined had cried, attacking from behind. After laying him gently down on the sand, she'd knelt beside him and quietly pointed out his use of an incorrect pejorative. As he lay there battling tears, turning his surprisingly sweet submissive gaze up at her, she'd had such a vision of his future of panic, evasion, pain, and denial that she'd hugged him and let him up. He'd limped away in the wake of his fleeing friends and then he'd turned to jerk his middle finger in her direction.

"Dyke!"

"Keep it up, kid," laughed Billie. She liked a boy who was willing to learn and had a bit of spirit, especially when he's headed for trouble.

.

Even Crispin's caught up in it and he's American and doesn't understand cricket at all. Australia needs one run to draw level and two runs to win. The batsman sweats in the center of the great big oval, bowed under the weight of his countrymen's unreasonable expectations.

"Bet you ten dollars he's out next ball," says Billie.

"You're on," says her mother.

"Sssh," says Crispin, unexpectedly. Billie looks at him and laughs. A pity because she misses the next ball, which does indeed do what she'd predicted.

"Oh, poor man," says Heather.

"What a loser," says Crispin.

"Well, he tried, that's the main thing."

"No it isn't," says Billie, bored by little Aussie battlers.

"Winning isn't everything."

"Yes it is," says Crispin.

The screen is filled with exuberant West Indians jumping about. Billie feels tears coming on. She finds success inexplicably moving.

"What are you, kid? A witch or what?" Crispin wants to know, as Heather fumbles in her fringed suede handbag, finds a ten-dollar note, and hands it to Billie. "You sure put a hex on the poor guy. How'd you tell?"

"A failure of nerve," says Billie. "The Cinderella complex. On some level he wanted to lose. I could see it in his shoulders."

"His shoulders." Crispin straightens his own.

Heather could get very upset at this point. She decides not to because she always feels so beaten-up afterward. It seems to her there's a new brutalism at large in the world.

There's a community meeting in the Long House this evening, concerning the forming of teams to attack the lantana that's spreading over the land, strangling everything that's good and natural and native. Heather had thought she'd skip it but now she changes her mind. Someone has to stand up for Australia.

The successful, opportunistic lantana is a metaphor, really, thinks Heather as she listens to her two very own lantanas happily chatting away in the corner. She takes a step back, as it were, which is not easy when it comes to those you've given birth to. Narrow-eyed, she maps a future where Billie strides about the planet as though it were a giant playground designed only for her amusement and material advancement. Come to think of it, her own mother had been a bit like that, heavily into the acquisition of pop-up toasters, vertical grillers, and other minor electrical appliances. A smaller frame of reference, perhaps, but the same symptoms. They do say character traits often skip a generation.

There's a photo of Heather on the bamboo bookshelf, taken a quarter of a century ago at an anti–Vietnam War rally. It had been printed in the *Toowoomba Chronicle*. In it, she wears a T-shirt which reads MAKE LOVE, NOT WAR. Heather's proud of this picture and all it stands for, but all Billie said when she saw it was "God, you've aged so much. It's amazing." And not a word about the issues.

Heather remembers a quarrel they had once when she was staying at Billie's place in Sydney. The Gulf War had just finished. They'd been standing in a back lane at midnight in Glebe wrestling over a garbage bin. Heather had wanted to know why Billie didn't put the bottles, tins, and newspapers out separately for collection. Billie'd muttered that she couldn't be bothered.

"Why ever not?" her mother had cried.

"What's the point?"

Heather had launched into a treatise on the necessity for recycling, most of which Billie'd already read in the leaflet the council had left in the mailbox. She really hadn't wanted to go through it all again.

"Mum," she'd wailed, "there are five hundred oil wells blazing in Kuwait and you're still fussing about putting the bottles out. The world's so dumb and you're so . . . so . . ." Unable to control the fact that she sounded and felt like a twelve-year-old, Billie had decided to go the whole way: "and you're so dumb too. Face it, Mum. The whole world's fucked. It's not my fault."

Heather had felt teary then and she feels teary now. Why can't she have a daughter who, for instance, is volunteering to go to—well, you name it, there are plenty of places to choose from—instead of one whose main concern is getting to Byron Bay to do some surfing and hang out with her friends and who, in the instant future like now, was intent on persuading Crispin to come with her to the Bellingen pub for a drink. Crispin, she notes, is immediately persuaded.

"You'll come, won't you, babe? We'll take the ute."

"Thank you, no," says Heather, rising from her cushions—oh God, that awful stiffness she suffers nowadays. Perhaps she should abandon cushions and get what Billie would call a proper chair. "There's a community meeting I should attend."

Heather does not see, though she can perfectly imagine, the swiftly smothered flicker of amusement that passes between Crispin and Billie. Feeling sad, she exits.

"Looks like we'll have to take your bike," says Crispin happily. His words float to her through the open doorway. Heather raises her eyes to heaven and immediately feels affirmed. It's a fine velvet night, no question about it—so velvety, in fact, that you could take it in your hands and run its smoothness through your fingers; so fine you could take a handful and thread it through your wedding ring if you had one. Moonlight streams like milk from a bottle, all over the yurt. Well, on the face of it you'd have to say the world's worth saving, wouldn't you?

•

𝕵n the pub Billie finds herself discussing this very subject with a koala bear who's clutching a bucket of money it's taken all day at the shopping mall to collect. The talk has turned green. The koala bear says it wants to save the planet for its children, and its children's children.

Billie thinks that hidden inside all the fake fur is a cowardly conservative devoid of imagination and entirely lacking in the natural desire to see what comes next. This bloody bear would probably have given the wheel the thumbs-down if it had been around at the time.

"Ever heard of evolution?"

"Yes," says the mummy bear.

"Well, maybe green is not the fittest color. What's so great about green? Maybe green is not a color destined to survive. Why not redecorate?"

"Tangerine people and marmalade skies," croons Crispin, who remembers a time when the world was much more colorful. The koala bear decides Crispin is a passé person and says it is worried about its children and has to go home. Billie offers a lift, which the bear accepts because she's been on her feet all day. Because she's had a bit to drink and she thinks the gesture would please her mother, Billie chucks in the ten dollars she won from Heather, grabs the bucket, and has a quick whip round the bar before leaving.

When they get to the bear's place, she asks Billie in for a cup of decaf and Billie accepts. Once indoors the bear sheds her suit and turns out to be a short plump young woman called Amber. She picks her way through a litter of toys to put the kettle on. While waiting for it to boil Amber tips the contents of the bucket onto the table and counts the day's takings. Two small boys are trying to kill each other in the corner. One punches the other in the stomach, a low blow that apparently the recipient doesn't consider reasonable.

"Why'd you do that?"

"Because you just don't see. You just never get it, do you?"

Billie wonders if perhaps the whole family is mad. She wonders if it wouldn't be a good idea to submit all would-be breeders to a test.

"Not bad," says Amber. "If you work it out that's about ten dollars an hour, tax-free."

"The bears'll be grateful."

"Bugger the bears. This is for me and the kids. Have you ever tried to live on the single parent's allowance?"

"No."

"No. Well, if you had you'd know what it felt like to be an endangered species."

The boys in the corner munch on each other's limbs. Billie feels like asking for her money back. In theory Billie knows she shouldn't be judgmental, but she finds she is, so she quickly gulps her coffee and leaves.

On the way back to the pub to collect Crispin, Billie plays with the idea that, once we've fucked it up to the point where all the seas turn purple, the rivers cease to run, and all the stars fall down, a compact snarling multitoothed androgynous creature could come sliding out from a dark crevice and take over the planet. Before she can explore this further, here's Crispin in the main street, leaning against a phone booth, having a quiet smoke. As she slows down he flicks the butt into the road in a somersault of sparks and smiles. He's handsome, thinks Billie, in a black-and-white movie sort of way. She can understand what her mum sees in him. What would Heather think of Rosie, should they meet? Heather's bound to like her. She accepts everyone. Billie feels obscurely robbed that her mother hadn't made a fuss when she'd told her she was gay. In the face of the coming-out dramas her friends described, Billie felt pale and insignificant.

Crispin straddles the bike and she takes him back to Bundagen, where they find that Heather's still out so they walk in

the bright night through the small banana plantation and the
mango trees and across the grassy cliff tops to the beach where,
hand in hand on the edge of the sand, they dance by the light
of the moon.

"I wish I had a tail," says Billie. "I've always wanted one,
ever since I can remember," and she drapes her imaginary tail
elegantly over her arm to keep it out of the water.

·

"Who'd have thought it," says Crispin. He and Heather stand
side by side watching Billie pull away down the dusty track.

"Thought what?"

"That I'd be sorry to see her go."

Heather wipes away a tear. She counts this visit a success,
though she wishes she didn't find Billie so difficult. Crispin's
advice was to relax and not to take it so seriously but that's his
advice for everything—though he never follows it himself.

Crispin tells her the story about the single parent in the
koala suit.

"I think the kid was quite shocked," he said, and Heather's
glad to hear it, taking it as a sign of her having done something right in the raising of Billie.

"Still and all," adds Crispin, "it's a quick way of raising a
few bucks when things get tough."

Heather agrees. There've been times in her life when she
wished she had that kind of nerve.

Crispin says he ought to be getting back to tend his wasabi.

He has no intention of getting roped in on any lantana struggles that may be pending. They're all mad. It's much too hot. Heather smiles, slides her arms round his neck, and kisses him.

"Run along then, sweetheart," she says. He feels dismissed. Usually she'd pout a bit, especially when she suspects he's ducking out of doing his bit, but she's very sunny today. He puts this down to Billie's departure but the truth is, last night, a bare handful of yards from where Billie and Crispin were playing, Heather and a newcomer to the land, a lovely youth called—but she's forgotten what he's called, which for some reason makes her feel even better—had lain themselves down on a fine unmarked mattress of a sand dune and made love.

The feel of that fit and finely muscled body holding hers, the gorgeous young smell of his skin, had made her more aroused than she'd felt for years. This boy had smelled of honey and thyme and, yes, the other sort of time too. He'd had all the time in the world for sweetness and he'd shared some of it with her, leaving an aura of pleasure that lingered. She'd taken this boy in like medicine, an elixir. Not that she yearned for her own youth back. Life's a journey with a beginning, middle, and end and no regrets, no hormone replacement therapy, and, should she have the misfortune to come to that, no chemo-therapy either. Heather's a strong woman. It takes courage to go gently but, as Heather might tell you, any other approach is a noisome waste of time.

After the funeral, Rosemary walks home from Waverley Cemetery, which is only a skip and a hop from where she lives, though this afternoon all Rosemary's managing is a markedly leaden walk. Why are we born, why do we live as we do, behave as we do, work as we do, love as we do, and after all that die as we do?

These weary whys and what-fors trundle their dull circle in her head with the answers as remote as is usual in these cases unless the divine intervenes. The afternoon sky is splendid, but it bears no sign of revelation. She stops, stands on top of a cliff that is a perilous jigsaw of eroded boulders, and looks down on the ocean bursting in great white blossoms at its foot. In her hand she holds an alarmingly fat book. It is a proof copy of *The Witching Hour* by Fiona Faraday, and it is about the menopause. Fiona had given it to her this morning at the house before the funeral. Rosemary's been lugging it about all day. Somehow, being given a book on menopause at a funeral seems like catching the bride's bouquet at a wedding—you're next. She's tempted to hurl the book into the waves but the cumbersome respect she has for the written word prevents her. She knows she'll read it because she feels she must, just as she knows she will send a polite note of congratulation to its author when she has done so.

The boys remain packed round the video game outside the laundromat. Rosemary stops and watches for a moment.

"Yes," yelp the boys, jumping up and down, greeting victories she cannot see, their voices on an upward scale, "yeah yeah yeah yeah yeah yeah yeah yeah yes!"

Where are the girls, what do they do, and where do they spend their time? Rosemary sees the park from her windows, she sees the beach, and she sees the sea; she sees boys taking up space in these public places with their games and pursuits but rarely does she see girls.

She's supposed to be going line dancing tonight at the Imperial Hotel in Erskineville but she's not in the mood and besides, it's been so long she's afraid she's forgotten how to do it. Instead she phones those involved, makes her excuses, and, armed only with a Wettex, goes in search of decay.

She cleans windows and then scours the bath, the lavatory and basin with a nonscratch foaming cleaning product. Pursued by mortality Rosemary washes floors and waxes them, cleans out the refrigerator, straightens all of the cutlery in all of its drawers, and then sits on the pretty pale blue boards of her kitchen floor and considers the disturbed and astonished Kristeva, who knows something's up but not, exactly, what. Rosemary scoops her up, grabs the Petgloss, and plunges her, complaining, into the bath.

Daphne told Rosemary once how the psychotherapist she was seeing had advised her to get plenty of exercise because physical activity caused the brain to produce its own antidepressant drug. For her part Rosemary knows that when her house is in order her mind will surely follow, and, indeed, when Rosemary casts herself down on her bed and the damp, forgiving cat comes and sits on Rosemary's stomach and starts to knead with those spiky little paws of hers, Rosemary does feel as though she's pushed back the black borders a bit.

The Witching Hour winks at her from a high shelf. She tips Kristeva onto the floor, takes it down, holds it at arm's length, rallies her fading eyesight, and begins. The phone rings. It's Billie. It must be Billie. It certainly should be Billie. It isn't. It's Daphne, who's calling to tell her that the notebooks are proving a disappointment.

"Listen to this," instructs Daphne. " 'Another warm day. Busy in office. Sat late when all had gone—how these dowdies do dawdle and prevaricate—reading papers to avoid crowds on omnibus. Came home.' And then the next day, which is a Saturday. 'Woke early, hoping for fine day. Raining. Birdbath full of droppings. Must clean. Mother reads aloud *The Times*' obituaries she's been saving up all week. Cooked us a chop.' There's pages like this. Days, weeks, months, years. What does any of it tell us?"

"That she was busy, lonely, bored. Sounds like a description for any one of us at times."

"At times, yeah, okay. But decade after decade, and in code. Why? And in all that, just one mention of my mother. Yet she wrote to bloody Ethel all the time, and the old cow wrote back too, I'm sure. Well, I'm reasonably sure. As you know, when Isobel went up in flames she took every piece of paper she could lay her hands on with her."

"What was the reference?"

There is a long silence.

"Daphne?"

"Hang on. Yes. This is what she says, the only reference in all those tedious jottings. Listen. 'An aerogramme from my young stray today, posted to the office. The stray, it seems, has been led astray, giving birth to a daughter some months back. What is to become of them? She can hardly hope to support both herself and her child by her writing and she has managed to quarrel with anyone who might have been persuaded to assist her.' Then it's back to the burnt chops and bird shit." Daphne's voice is choppy with dismay.

"I'm sorry. I wish you were here. You definitely sound in need of a hug." And so, thinks Rosemary, does Isobel, fire-eater, trapeze artist, writer, mother, and misfit.

"Thanks. I just feel the whole thing's been a waste of time."

"What's left that could shed some light?"

"Well, there's Edith Black's old house in the Blue Mountains. Haven't they turned it into a writer's center or something? It might contain some clue. Though actually some of Black's own diary entries are distressing enough. 'Spent all afternoon cleaning the kitchen cupboards,' for example. 'At 4 P.M. the fog rolled in. Wrote and posted a letter to Mother. V. tired.' Isobel used to take me up there, in the summer, when I was little. I have dim recollections of women in hats sitting under trees and buzzing away like bees. It's not far from your place, you know."

Rosemary does know. She also knows what's coming, and it does. "So when are you going up to your house?"

"Saturday morning."

"That's too soon for me."

"Well, that's all right. Come up when you're ready."

"Great. I will. It'll be good. We can wander round a bit. Get the feel of the place."

"Spend a few afternoons cleaning the kitchen cupboards." This task had been part of Rosemary's plans. She keeps quiet about her recent cleaning binge.

"V. funny. I'll come up on the train and I'll bring my bike. How's that?"

Rosemary, contemplating the surprising fact that Daphne owns such a thing as a bike, says nothing for a second.

"Okay?" prompts Daphne.

"That's fine." And probably it will be. Rosemary's very fond of Daphne really and she can't help thinking it'll be good for her to get out in the fresh air for a while. Rosemary pushes away the thought that wherever Daphne goes the air is unlikely to stay fresh for long.

•

*L*orraine left her leg in San Francisco, which, as she likes to say these days, was a blessing in disguise. It put a stop to all her boozing, running round, and womanizing. It started her on the path to wisdom, financial success, and pointed her toward permaculture. In short, thinks Lorraine, as she sits fingering the pretty, naked inspector for the National Parks and Wildlife Service who sighs and squirms on her large lap, the Goddess works in mysterious ways, etc. Lorraine's always been crazy for girls in uniform and this one's something else, this girl's gorgeous—this girl shaves it and Lorraine loves girls who do, girls with velvety clefts neat and sweet as almonds like this one that is about to split and offer it all up softly but, holy mother of God, who's this tearing up the driveway on a machine so beautiful it sends tingles all through Lorraine from the top of her crewcut head to the toes of her phantom foot and causes her fingers to falter so the pretty blond person in her lap sighs harder and sobs slightly and begs her not to stop, but Lorraine must because her old friend Billie has arrived to pay her a visit.

"Don't go, girl," whispers Lorraine, as the bike stops in front of the verandah and the engine cuts, leaving a hot ticking noise as the metal rearranges itself in the warm night. "Please, please don't walk out on me until I give you what you need. Go to the cabin and lie down because I'm going to come and take care of it like it's never been taken care of before." Will she, won't she—she does. The doll, the darling. It'll be seriously rough talk and nipple rings next.

"Billie. Billie, yo Bill. Oh kid, it's good to see you," and the friends come together, a quiet clash of leather in the night. When they've sorted themselves out and settled down with beers and a joint on the verandah, they have a lot to talk about. It's been ages.

"It has, it has indeed. There's been some changes with you, I can see. Where's the nose ring?"

"In my pocket." Billie's been meaning to put it back in all day but she hasn't had a chance. She knew Lorraine would pick up on it immediately. She'd given it to her, after all. She finds it, holds it out. "Here. Fix it for me." Lorraine does. "Better.

You were starting to look a tad straight. Growing your hair, I see. Who is she?"

Billie sucks smoke, smiles, and does not answer. Later.

"Aren't my guests good. They're all in bed. Well, the one in number 4 is always in bed, but his nurse says he's asleep." Napoleon, the nurse in question, comes out of the cabin where his charge lies sleeping and slips naked into the pool. Their conversation is punctuated by his laps and splashes.

Lorraine runs Wagon Wheels with her partner, Liz. They do it month and month about so that neither gets burnout. In their months off, each goes far away and forgets it. It's a demanding place. Someone died here last week.

"I hate it when they do. It's a good place to die, and I'm pleased for that, but still, I'm not Mother Teresa, suffering gives me no pleasure. Each time it happens it knocks me about. You staying long, or what?"

"I don't know."

"Hey, it's okay. Nobody's scheduled to die in the next little while. In fact, we've got quite a few straight dyke bookings over the next few weeks. Honeymoon couples and that sort of thing. All hot and happy. You can sashay in and out every morning, give them breakfast in bed. You'll love it."

"I should use a phone."

"Sure. In the office."

Billie gets up, goes through the door behind them and finds the phone. She dials Rosemary's number. The line's busy. She pushes the redial button a couple of times and it stays busy.

Billie puts down the receiver, looks round the room. Motorbike girl posters still, including that antique Marianne Faithfull one with the roses. Oh shit, no. Billie looks at herself, blue-tacked to the wall, and here she is sixteen again, and it's summer holidays so she's hanging out with friends and it's one particular day, the day she'd been smoothly cruised by Lorraine while waiting at a bus stop. Billie'd known exactly what this woman was about, the quick wordless contact that went unnoticed by her friends and was filed away by Billie for future reference.

Lorraine had been working on a road gang that summer, the one before she went to America, standing in the sun all day in frayed cutoffs and a luminous orange vest, swiveling a lollipop-shaped sign with SLOW written on one side and STOP on the other. Boring work, lots of time to think, but Lorraine knew it wasn't wise to think too much about randy schoolgirls who followed her about because the world did not take kindly to it, though why the world should care when both parties were willing was beyond fathoming. At some point, though, Lorraine had popped Billie into her babydoll pajamas, posed her on her sleek machine, and taken a few snaps. Babydolls. Billie cannot imagine a time when she possessed any such garment but she must've because there's the proof right there on the wall.

Lorraine'd told Billie she was going down to Sydney for the gay and lesbian Mardi Gras. Billie'd begged to go with her. Lorraine'd said, "Only if you get a note from your mum," and Billie'd said, "No problem," and so it had proved. The problem had come later, with Billie back at school at the start of junior year, when the word was out about her marching in the parade under the banner OUT OF THE CLOSET AND INTO THE CLASSROOM. Then the whispering and the avoiding started. Junior year was pure hell, one bright spot being a postcard from Lorraine from some place Billie'd never been but was certainly going to one day. There were lots of things Billie was going to do one day and sex was one of them. It didn't seem reasonable to be pilloried for something you'd never done and Billie hadn't, though she'd thought about it lots lying on the lawn late at night while possums ground their teeth in the gum tree. The school's top surfer had done it, which was good because she'd helped take some of the heat off Billie by getting pregnant and providing everyone with another topic for conversation.

By senior year everyone was bored with the queer question and jaded by sex in general, finding better things to think about. Billie'd capped her school career by taking a girl to the end-of-year formal. They weren't an item, but who was to know? Holding hands they took to the dance floor. The school band, never accurate at the best of times, fumbled a few beats. Billie's heart kept pace with the faltering drum. Two boys had joined them, then two other girls. The band picked up the pace and so the love that dare not speak its name shyly circled the gym to a few derisive cheers, three wolf whistles, and a splash of unnoticed tears from the coach of the rugby league team, which was peculiar but then so was he, though he never would admit it.

There was a story going round about how one Saturday after

the game the coach had walked into the changing rooms and found two of his star players sitting on the bench with the ice packs kept for treating bruises wrapped round their pricks.

"What do you think you're doing?" inquired the coach.

"Ah, we all know how you like to grab a couple of cold ones after the game," they'd said, though when it came to what happened next, opinions varied.

Billie can't call Rosie now, not with memories whispering like so many dead leaves in the corner, not with the girl-self on the wall staring at her in what strikes Billie now as pure confusion and an uncomfortable degree of bravado. It's mad, but she feels stranded in a no-woman's-land between then and now and can't find her feet or her tongue. She'll ring later, from her cabin. Then she remembers that only Lorraine's cabin has a phone. She tries again but Rosemary's line's still busy. For some reason Billie thinks of phone sex, which could certainly tie up the line. Doesn't sound a lot of fun to Billie, but when you're older it might. Still, the thought of Rosie talking dirty down the line to a stranger is intriguing.

The nurse must be out of the pool. Billie can hear the murmur of voices out on the verandah, his high and stressed, Lorraine's reassuring. Billie wonders what exactly happened to Lorraine that made her so good at all this nurturing stuff. She must've seen the light, like St. Paul on the road to Damascus. There's a soft knock on the back door of the office. Billie opens it.

"Hi, I'm Melissa."

"Melissa. Hi. I'm Billie." Billie holds out her hand and Melissa shakes it.

"You staying here?"

"Well . . . I . . . she told me to wait. Only I got a cramp."

"Is that you, hon? Come here. And Billie . . . what are you up to? Still on the phone?"

Billie and Melissa go out onto the verandah just as Napoleon the nurse is summoned by the bedside bell in Cabin 4. Melissa, now she's cooled off a bit, thinks she should go home or her husband will be worried. Lorraine accompanies her to her car, whirring along in her wheelchair. The underwater lights in the pool go out, dark water slaps the sides. Billie peels off her leathers and slips into it, relaxes, and sinks right down to the bottom, stays there for a slow count of ten, then shoots up fast to find Lorraine sitting on the edge dangling her foot in the water.

"What was that about?" meaning Melissa.

"Dunno. Never did find out. An hour ago I was ready to marry her, except it turns out she's married already." Lorraine laughs. "Win some, lose some. What can you do? Now come on, kid," tossing Billie a towel, "get out of there, mix us a drink, there's tequila in the freezer, and tell me all about her." So Billie does. And when Billie's finished her story Lorraine asks what it is Rosemary does for a living because Billie hasn't said.

"She's an associate professor of early childhood studies."

"You must come in very handy then," says Lorraine.

To change the subject Billie asks Lorraine what it was that changed her from who she was to who she is.

"I saw the light," roars Lorraine, who never ceases to be amused at her fate. "Honest, it sounds mad, but I did. I was on the operating table. They were, you know . . ."—Lorraine's hand makes a sawing motion in the empty air where her leg had been—"and suddenly I wasn't there. I was in a long dark tunnel struggling toward a perfect circle of light. It took some big fat effort I can tell you, but finally pant pant, groan moan there I was and it was so peaceful and gentle and . . . like floating and free, no gravity, nothing like that, and I was happy to be there and I'm floating round twittering and wittering like a new-hatched thing when it's like a force grabs me, pushing me back toward the tunnel. It wasn't exactly rough, it was tender really, if that makes any sense, but it was firm at the same time and somehow I understood that I'd turned up early for this particular appointment, there'd been some mistake and it wasn't time for me to be there. So I just, you know, picked myself up, brushed myself off and walked back down that tunnel with a cheery wave and lay back down on the operating table and nobody knew I'd been anywhere except me. And now you. And Carmen. I told her. I thought a Koori would understand, the way they go on all the time, but I could tell she thought I was crazy. What about you? Doesn't matter if you don't believe me. I know it's true."

"I knew something awesome had happened."

"Awesome. Exactly. Picked on by the divine. Then I had to

find a reason. In the end it was easy, because as I healed and went back into the world I saw everything from a different perspective."

"You mean a religious perspective?"

"No. More practical than that. Because of the way I got dragged along by the truck there was a lot of damage and they'd had to take the leg off really high, so there was no question of fitting a prosthesis. I had to settle for a wheelchair. Everything changed. The world was wrong. Things were all in the wrong place; things I never used to give a second's thought to became a nightmare. Sure, I could adapt my own environment but then what was I supposed to do, stay hidden away inside it? No way. I had this idea then of starting a holiday resort with everything designed from scratch, not modified, but architect-designed by the best people without any compromise. I talked to people. I nagged people, and when it came to the crunch I straight out guilt-tripped people into investing. None of them regret it, I'm happy to say. I found this land, which everyone said was low-grade. Found an architect. Built the first cabin. It all tumbled into place from there—the permaculture thing to improve land quality, which it did, the medical cabin so the really sick could come somewhere beautiful, the courses in Koori culture filled up every other week. I'm making a fortune. Eight cabins. Booked all year. Not just wheelies, but lesbians and gays too. There's money in being politically correct. Sorry, kid. I do go on. You're looking a bit glazed. Anyway, next time I hope he lets me stay."

"He?"

"Bad luck, Billie. God's a bloke. I've been there. I know."

"How do you know? I thought you didn't see anyone, it was just a golden glow and an invisible force."

"Right. But only a bloke would shove you about like that." Lorraine laughs. Billie doesn't. She can't believe Lorraine believes any of it. Perhaps the accident had caused some brain damage.

"Come on, Billie, lighten up. You take everything so seriously. You asked me what happened and I told you. Whoever or whatever it was did me a good turn. Hell, it was probably just the anesthetic."

Lorraine takes herself to the top of the ramp leading down to the pool. She takes herself out of the electric wheelchair, sheds her clothes, and flops into one of the plastic chairs lined up by the water. Lorraine glides gently down into the pool, abandons the chair, and bobs around. The water's half-chlorinated, half-salt, which makes it easier to float. Knowing Billie's unhappy about something and knowing she can always be distracted by a game of more or less anything, Lorraine grabs a ball and throws it. Billie throws it back and dives in.

Later though, tucked between crisp sheets, Billie thinks about it. She wishes she'd never asked Lorraine what had happened. She hates that sort of story. It belongs with flying saucers on terrible American television programs made to keep credulous idiots amused. It's not what she expected from a woman she's admired and respected since she was practically a child. But Billie's no longer a child and she's ashamed at this childish disappointment she's feeling and her almost petulant resentment at having to rethink Lorraine's part in her life. Mentors are easy to deal with, it's all one-way traffic, but now Lorraine's proved to be imperfect and Billie must either rework her into a friend or fade her out. Unable to sleep Billie gets up, finds pen and paper, and writes a sexy letter to Rosemary. She thinks Rosemary's probably gone to her house in the mountains by now so she will send it there.

.

"Critical mass is the minimum amount of radioactive material necessary to produce a nuclear reaction."

"Yeah? Coffee?"

"Please. The main point is, once critical mass has been reached, the process becomes self-sustaining," continues Billie, who has the bit lodged firmly in her teeth along with various bits of the bacon they've just had for breakfast. "Everyone's into it at the moment, right across the field. Life's full of situations where a process becomes self-sustaining after some threshold point has been reached. The problem is, what's the magic number? How many people are necessary before an innovation becomes an accepted part of life?"

Lorraine and Billie drink their coffee by the pool. Billie is focused on her future. Mangoes plop from the trees. Departing guests wheel luggage to their cars. Those who are staying breakfast on verandahs, planning the day. The soothing hum of well-oiled wheels places the morning firmly on track. Cabin 4 shows no sign of activity but everything's cool, Lorraine's checked.

"And how many women are senior partners in law firms at the moment?"

"Between five and fifteen percent."

"Is that a critical mass?"

"It could be. In a sociological context research shows the threshold for critical mass can range from as little as five percent. Anyway, the percentage is getting higher. More women than men are doing law at university now."

"Ha!"

"What do you mean, Ha!?"

"Why are more women than men doing law?"

"Times change."

"No, they don't. The only reason more women are doing law or any other thing is that law doesn't matter anymore. The men have moved on and you can bet wherever they've moved to, that's where the power is."

"Well, where are they?"

"I don't know. How would I? I'm just busy carving out my tiny corner of life."

"*Cherchez les garçons,* then."

"Exactly."

"Where the boys are, that's where I want to be," wails Billie, producing quite a creditable tremolo.

"Hey. Not bad. Who sang that anyway? Annette Funicello, Sandra Dee, who?"

"Not k.d. lang, that's for sure."

Lorraine emits a low growl.

"Do you think it's true that she was on with Martina?"

"Jeez, I hope so. Us lifestyle icons should stick together."

An old blue Valiant roars in, the kind with the push-button gear change. On top of it are two surfboards. Inside it are Marsha and Carmen, poor but gorgeous, come to collect Billie and take her for a surf.

•

The sea's turned red in the night. There's a rubbish truck parked outside the fish and chips shop. Shattered saints spill down onto the street. It seems a good time to leave and Rosemary intends to as soon as she can catch Kristeva who has hidden herself, despite her careful cat-fooling efforts as she prepared for departure. Kristeva hates the car.

Helicopters come in low to chop, chatter, and circle the beach. People run back and forth across the park, stand at the ocean's edge, their jaws slack with wonder. Members of the surf club blow whistles and warn everyone to stay out of the water. The brave and hideous boys scream and laugh and hurl themselves off the rocks. A dead sea turtle drifts in and lands belly-up on the sand. Before the Man from ORCA can appear to give it mouth-to-mouth resuscitation, someone scoops it up and takes it home to use as an ashtray.

Rosemary looks through the crowd for any sign of Theresa. She asks the driver of the rubbish truck but he'd been given the address by a real estate agent with the instruction to empty the place. He thought the occupant must have had quite a party before she moved out because everything had been broken and thrown about.

Rosemary enters the empty flat. Pale patches on the floor, made by saintly feet, and a few bits of bright coral mosaic and crushed abalone shell from the hem of Saint Hildegarde's gown are all that's left of Theresa's devotional Disneyland. Rosemary finds herself looking for a note, an explanation, though she knows this is foolish. Theresa didn't like her, after all, so she wouldn't feel compelled to keep Rosemary informed of her movements. The rubbish removalist comes in.

"That's it then, is it?" He looks round and decides he's right but he's not. Rosemary has just seen a small figure, intact, on the mantelpiece. She moves herself between him and it.

"Looks like it."

The rubbish man looks at Rosemary. It looks as if he has something more to say, but if he does he's changed his mind.

"Okay. Well, close the door behind you when you go."

"Yes."

The rubbish man nods, walks to the doorway. *"Dominus vobiscum,"* he says with a wink, and is gone.

Rosemary picks up the figurine. Is this one of the tiny Nuns of the Incarnation? No, it's Our Lady again, six inches tall, perched on a cloud, rays emanating from the palm of each outstretched hand. Rosemary takes her to the window. She is beautifully made, the porcelain flawless, the colors clear and bright. Rosemary can see no maker's mark. Had Theresa hidden herself away in this malodorous flat in order to create her saints and cultivate her own cult? Rosemary knew that in the early days of the church, before the men took over and bullied everyone into straight lines, there had been a multiplicity of saints with their factions and followers. Christianity might have developed into a kind of Hinduism with a whole host of crowd-pleasing and exotic deities.

Rosemary wishes she'd been able to see the whole collection outside in the daylight. The fabulous thing, and Rosemary can't think why she hadn't noticed this immediately, is that there hadn't been a single male among them, not one matted beard and no crosses, no crucifixes, no thorns or bloody-browed bleeding Jesuses anywhere in sight.

Rosemary can't believe they've gone. What blackness had taken hold of their creator to bring about such destruction? She wants to see the female saints resurrected. She sees them gleaming, dotted round the rock pool. Glorious girls with lapis eyes, dear little ears inlaid with mother-of-pearl, garments dotted with garnet, hair festooned with purest pearls, beach towels draped over their arms. A beach needs a few saints, thinks Rosemary, slipping the tiny virgin into her pocket. Now she should go but there's something else, she's sure there is, so she continues her search and in the bathroom she finds it writ large and rainbow bright on the wall.

I will not have you converse with men but with angels

which sounds all right to Rosemary, who has always, since early childhood, secretly believed angels to be girls, even if they were called Michael and Gabriel.

•

*L*orraine wheels herself quietly beneath creaking trees along smooth tracks laid in the surrounding bush. She's checking her nature trails to make sure nothing has fallen across them to obstruct her guests. She's half hoping she'll find Melissa where she'd found her yesterday, with her cute bum in the air as she admired some rare native orchid or other, for the regeneration of which she apparently held Lorraine entirely responsible. Lorraine hadn't liked to say how they'd smothered clumps of them with concrete when the paths had gone in. She'd smiled a humble smile and murmured something about Mother Nature.

Today in the same spot a fine black snake flows across the path. She watches, envying the snake its neat and limbless condition. She doesn't know what if anything it means to have a black snake cross your path. Good luck, bad luck, or nothing in particular? Because the thing is, she's definitely getting a peculiar feeling. Like someone's left a tap on or a plug out causing something somewhere to seep away to do a lot of secret damage. Like someone somewhere—no, not somewhere, but close—is running out of luck.

Lorraine doesn't believe any of this, and she has no wish to slander or further stereotype any long-suffering and misunderstood snake but the fact is, as she glides away, the feeling winds along behind. She checks the obvious candidate for disaster but the boy in Cabin 4 is fine today, or as fine as can be reasonably expected, and then this and that happens, things get busy, and gradually Lorraine's foreboding fades.

·

*T*he phone rings in the empty house. Kristeva's ears twitch. A fly buzzes. The dishwasher finishes its cycle. The answering machine picks up the call. Billie, deciding she'll ring later, doesn't leave a message. When Rosemary comes back she immediately checks the machine. Two messages. Nothing from Billie. Rosemary feels lonely. What she wants most is someone right here right now to talk to about saints and the menopause while the red sea churns beyond the windows. *The Witching Hour* sits beside the phone, although Rosemary's reasonably sure she didn't leave it there. Can this book walk or what? Suddenly Rosemary can't wait to get up to the mountains and read it and think about death and decay and all the things that ail her. Perhaps when she's faced it she can forget it and get on with her life. But first she must find an explanation for the uncommon state of the ocean. The surf club seems a good place to start. Rosemary places Our Lady on the marble ledge beneath the French early-nineteenth-century neoclassical mirror that fills a large part of one wall. She looks right at home there; indeed Rosemary fancies a quick look of complicity passes between them as if to say that the Virgin Mary too would have adopted the random-planet style of interior decoration favored by Rosemary if only she'd not had the misfortune to be married to a carpenter who'd insisted on making all the kitchen cupboards himself. Rosemary was prepared to bet Joseph had been the type who'd go on endlessly about the knots and whorls to be found in every bit of wood he laid hands on. She finds this attitude depressing. She finds wood depressing too. What is wood if not dull and some variation or another on the basic theme of brown? In Rosemary's opinion there are very few woods not greatly improved by a coat of paint.

.

Carmen, Marsha, and Billie stand at the top of the dunes watching wave after wave suck up into perfect juicy barrels. It couldn't be better.

"Hey. Let's get wet," yells Carmen, and they start to run. They stop at the water's edge. Billie zips her wet suit and fits on her fins. "Hey guys," she calls, falling on her board and smashing out into the white water, "take a good look at a quality left-hander."

Carmen laughs and follows. Marsha remains on the beach, fiddling with her fins. There's a lump in her throat she's trying to swallow because if she goes into the water with it she'll probably drown. She's got this thing about Billie; about the tilt of her head, her scowly look, long legs, and general air of swagger, and yes, Marsha has to admit, her propensity to be better at everything than anyone else. To prove the point Billie trims and cuts back into a sheer wall of water, raises her body, rears her handsome head over the tip of the board, shoots skyward, hits the lip of the wave, and flips over to hover gloriously in midair, giving gravity a good run for its money before she plummets, dragging Marsha's turbulent heart down with her into the foam.

And then there's nothing. Just cold salt water, smooth and round as a glass stopper, closing Billie's mouth.

.

"It's nature," says the leader of the lifesavers. "It's seaweed blossom, that's all it is. It happens every so often, when conditions favor it. It can't hurt you."

"Why are they so busily keeping everyone out of it, then?"

"People expect it. If we just left them to it, someone'd report us to the council."

Rosemary's tempted to sneak off round the corner and dip herself into the redness, but then she thinks she'd have to shower afterward and wash her hair and dry it, which all seems too much bother so she doesn't. She contents herself by walking back along the water's edge. A pink scum forms a fringe round her ankles, which she rinses off under one of the taps placed at the edge of the park for this purpose.

Crossing the road to the house Rosemary observes a thin trail of glitter running up the center of the street, marking the passing of the saints on their way to the tip. On the other side of this trail stands a short tense young woman in tight clothes who steps forward at Rosemary's approach. This is Yvonne who wanted the ride up to the commitment ceremony. Somehow, Rosemary's managed to forget all about this. She suggests Yvonne go and have a cup of coffee at the cafe while she goes upstairs to catch Kristeva and to pack a few things. These things will include the tiny virgin, *The Witching Hour,* a small blue glass jar of Neals Yard elderflower hand softener, and the reportedly sexy book she bought the other night because, distracted by death and menopause, she still hasn't found out how Blaize gets on with the woman with the Ray Bans, the state of the art sound system, and the blond curly hair. Now read on.

•

"*J* don't know why they call them mountains," grumbles Daphne. "They're not mountains at all. More like holes in the ground. I mean, how many mountains are there in the world you can stand and look down on?"

Rosemary and Daphne cling to the dizzying rail. Rosemary thinks of sudden cracks in the earth opening under her feet and clutches her friend's arm. Ever anxious to get on with it, Daphne had followed hot on Rosemary's heels and, upon arrival, insisted Rosemary drive her to this lookout point.

Daphne had crept off the train with her bags and her bike and a slightly exhumed look about her. She'd sniffed the air suspiciously.

"It stings," she'd said.

Daphne's a woman who likes to see what she's breathing. The crystalline morning disturbed. She lit a cigarette to restore balance. Immediately she'd been surrounded by strangers clamoring for a smoke.

"Really," she'd said. "Have you noticed? Ever since they made smoking a criminal activity you're accosted by the nicotine-starved every time you light up." In the car, peering suspiciously at passing scenery, Daphne had picked up her theme. "I nearly missed my train, too. This bloody taxi driver had the cheek to tell me I couldn't smoke in his cab, so I made him stop so I could get another one. Then he expected to be paid. Of course I refused. I tried to explain to him a few simple basics of contract law and how they applied in this situation, but you could tell it was all news to him. He started screaming and kicking my bike while I was trying to get it out of the trunk. I told him he should have a smoke and calm down, which was when he decided to chuck my suitcase into the gutter. The world's gone mad.

"Very nice," says Daphne, turning from the rail. "Let's go, shall we? They might shut." Actually Liquorland doesn't shut until nine on Fridays, but Rosemary's quite happy to leave the lookout. Sometimes she gets this strange feeling of wanting to jump when she's up high somewhere. The thought just saunters up from behind after a minute or two and casually suggests itself. She's learned to deal with it but nonetheless Rosemary is happy to leave the thought to gaze alone upon the mountains while she and Daphne flee toward the color and movement of Kmart.

•

While Daphne stocks up on the Bell's, Rosemary pops next door to buy a pound of frozen New Zealand flathead and some Ping-Pong balls for Kristeva.

A woman at the commitment ceremony had told Rosemary

how Katoomba Kmart is supposed to be a good pickup place for lesbian mothers on Monday mornings when they come in for the red light specials. Rosemary's thinking about what you might do with a lesbian mother on a Monday morning should you succeed in picking her up when she sees her friend Penelope, neither lesbian nor mother, standing with a loaded shopping cart in the no-man's-land between housewares and the deli counter. Something's not right. Penelope wears a distinctly Serbian expression and Rosemary can guess why. She looks round. She can't see him either. Why does Bruce vanish at the drop of a hat and, yet more puzzling—since everyone feels the need to escape their nearest and dearest now and again—how? In this case he probably took two steps back and one sideways and vanished down an aisle, which is easy enough in Kmart but it was a well-known fact that Bruce could do the same thing miles from anywhere without so much as a blighted spinifex for shelter.

Penelope and Rosemary glide along the aisles, cart to cart, eyes peeled for the missing one. They stop to peruse the cheeses.

"I think," says Penelope, picking up where they'd left off when last they'd seen each other, "at least it seems to me . . ."—Penelope pauses to flip a packet of Breton biscuits into her cart because she adores these with blue cheese—"that all those boys," and here she pauses to sigh, because it is sad, she thinks, a bit like the generation lost in the First World War, all those poets catching measles or mown down in mud, "and I've seen so many of them, you know . . . clever boys who sat down at nine o'clock one morning and lit a joint and before they knew it, a quarter of a century had gone past. And now where are they?"

"Missing in Kmart."

"It's not right though, is it?"

Penelope's reached the checkouts but Rosemary hangs back, sure she's forgotten something. She has. She leaves her cart full of the things she didn't come in for but is perfectly pleased to have, and hurries off to get Kristeva's Ping-Pong balls.

The store's about to close. People are milling about in the parking lot. Through the window she sees Bruce, buckling under the weight of twenty pounds of Pussy's Place, weaving his way to the car. The bag's got a hole in it.

It would, thinks Bruce, it's that kind of a day. It's always that kind of a day in the mountains. A line of grayish brown pellets marks his trail until mist rolls in and obscures it. Bruce chucks the depleted bag into the trunk and crawls into the passenger seat with a sigh.

"Fuss, fuss, fuss," he complains.

His back has never been good and moving up here hasn't improved it. He takes a joint out of the glove compartment and lights it. He finds a scuffed cassette of *Dido and Aeneas* on the floor, stuffs it into the slot, and settles back with a sigh. The tape loops, stretches, crackles, and finally comes across with the music. There is a rising rondo of purrs from the backseat.

.

*R*osemary makes a gin and tonic. Daphne pours a scotch, unpacks, and sets about sharpening a few pencils. There are times when Daphne's eyes glint with leaden determination like the sea on a dull morning.

"Bruce and Penelope have asked us for dinner," Rosemary tells her. Bruce and Penelope live just down the road. "Floryan will be there too. You should meet him. He's staying at the writer's center."

"Can he get me in there to look round?"

"I'm sure he can. It's more or less public property isn't it? I'm sure he'd be glad to show you around."

"People can be very weird about those things," meaning that she can and therefore expects all others to be the same.

"I suppose they can." Rosemary flaps the air with a tea towel to dispel the appalling smell made by flathead steaming on the stove. She switches off the stove, tells Kristeva she'll have to wait until the fish has cooled down, and takes her gin out into the garden where, inspecting a poorly pruned rose bush, she finds herself thinking about the secateurs murderer who snips off his victims' fingers in order to remove their rings in the safety of his own home. Rosemary gulps what remains of her drink and tips the shrunken ice cubes down onto stony ground. Tomorrow she will order a load of mushroom compost and a fifty-pound bag of Dynamic Lifter. Perhaps Daphne will feel moved to help shovel it, but then again perhaps she won't. Rosemary turns on the sprinklers and, moving to another part of the garden, begins deadheading the daisies while it is still light enough to do so.

"That was delicious," says Rosemary, referring to the pea and mushroom risotto, prepared by Penelope, which they've just eaten.

"Nothing beats a pea grown on the property," beams Penelope, pushing her empty plate from her. Despite her words and her clean plate, Penelope remains hungry. The golden skin of a good Welsh rarebit blisters seductively across her mind.

Bruce peers glumly into the bowl Daphne has just passed him. Since they moved to the mountains, he has grown resigned to finding flowers in the salad. He pushes a few nasturtium petals aside and helps himself to as small an amount of greenery as his wife will let him get away with. Penelope apparently believes anything green to be an indispensable factor in the attainment and maintenance of good health. Bruce pushes the leaves round his plate. He knows if he keeps up this display of enthusiasm and activity for long enough, she'll lose interest and he'll be able to quietly stuff the lot into the compost bucket where it belongs. Chervil, chives, arugula, baby leaves of English spinach, parsley, red and green mignonette lettuce—surely there must be a way to turn all this into a deeply nourishing and highly alcoholic liqueur and then everybody would be happy.

"Bad behavior," says Rupert, "is not always as amusing as all that. Pass that salad, there's a love." Bruce happily does so.

"But listen," insists Floryan, whose behavior it is that Rupert obliquely criticizes, "it gets so quiet up in that house I sometimes have to switch the copier on for company. No wonder I wank a lot. I've wanked in every room in the writer's center. I'm trying to cheer myself up."

Floryan has been in residence for a week. He has another week to go and intended to make the most of it but now this woman he's just met wants to come tomorrow morning to see the house. Well, Floryan doesn't care, it'll be a diversion. He'll organize morning tea and give her a tour pointing out the double bed with ME and YOU carved in the headboard. What Floryan wants to know is who was ME and who was YOU. Since this woman visited the house as a child, she might know. He'll show her the chair in the corner of the bedroom with the grubby upholstery no one can change because Edith Black herself chose the fabric, stitched the cover, and doubtless contributed to its grubbiness as well. He'll take her into the concrete and glass bunker in the garden where Edith wrote her books and where Floryan was trying to do the same in the chilly mossy silence at a table next to a glass case containing Edith's muskrat fur coat and gauntlet gloves that the authoress always put on before settling down to work—and no wonder, Floryan thinks, it's so damp and cold in here, even in summer, why on earth didn't the woman put in a fireplace? There's a plastic bowl piled with Ratsak in the corner and every morning the top layer of pellets has been taken during the night; Floryan, supposing this to be expected of whichever writer is in residence at the time, dutifully tips more in every morning. He is sure he can smell dead mice moldering under the floorboards. The worst bit, though, he'll save until last—the built-in standard British brolly-sized umbrella cupboard hidden in the wall next to the front door, designed and executed by Edith. Contemplating this unique piece of handiwork Floryan thought he at last understood the full and limitless horror of writer's block. Tottering on the edge of a black hole, he had slammed the door shut before he fell in. When he got his breath back, he had to admire the desperate ingenuity and strength of a mind that would rather tackle the tedium of building an umbrella cupboard than construct a simple sentence. Buoyed by the cheering fact that there's always someone worse off than yourself, Floryan had hurried across the lawn to the bunker to compose a few of his own. Writing is a life sentence, all right.

Looking round the table Floryan hopes someone will give him a ride back. He doesn't fancy walking back through the fog along the ill-lit streets where everyone looks like a serial killer. He noticed this the first day he'd arrived, the beanies and black balaclavas, the plaid shirts, bits of rope poking out from pants pockets. And now they're all going on about this secateurs murderer except Rupert, who leans over to Floryan and asks him what he thinks the expected shelf life of a relationship is these days.

"For me, you mean?"

"From your own experience, yes."

"On average?"

"Yes."

Floryan adds up a few numbers, divides the result by something, and says, "Eighteen hours."

Rupert nods thoughtfully. "Quite so," he says before turning away to talk to Penelope, leaving Floryan wondering what that was all about. By and large Floryan is not fond of queeny old actors, women writers, babbling dinner parties, these sodden misted mountains, and the whole fucking world, more or less. He's starting to resent having to deal with Daphne in the morning. He feels protective of Edith Black despite her mad cupboards and moth-eaten muskrat gauntlets. There was a pimple starting on his neck, just below his collar. He fingers it, dully battling the onset of discontent. He knows why he feels like this. His work isn't going well. The problem is his opening sentence. He keeps going back and changing it but still he's not happy. It has to do with the time his hero was four years old and saw his grandmother's cunt, but he can't get it right.

"I think it's tacky," says Rupert.

"What is?" snaps Floryan, thinking Rupert's read his mind and managed to put his fat finger precisely on the problem.

"This whole Mardi Gras thing. When I watch that parade I just wonder what they're doing. I can't identify at all. I like to think I belong to the human race, not to some subgroup enamored of frocks and sequins or leather jockstraps."

Floryan's inclined to agree. Not with the frock stuff—he likes to put on a good dress occasionally. It's fun and besides he looks better in a dress than do a hell of a lot of other people he could mention. What gets him down is this gay community business. He doesn't see how your sexual preference automatically makes you part of a community and certainly not a family, thank you very much. He flirts with the perilous thought that being gay must have been much more fun when it was illegal.

Then suddenly everyone at this table is talking about love. Daphne's telling them how she lived with this fellow for years and when it was over—though just when this was had been difficult to say and took months to decide, dragging on and on as these things tend to do—she left him and the next day he drank some kind of cleaning fluid because he'd read in a book how someone had killed himself this way and thought he'd give it a try. He hadn't died, though it was close. She went to visit him in the hospital afterward but now she thinks this was a mistake, though she doesn't say why. Then, about eight months later he'd shot himself, but by now Daphne can't be sure whether that act was connected to her or not.

"He must have loved you a lot," says Penelope cautiously.

"What nonsense," snaps Rupert. "That sort of thing's got nothing to do with love. It's something else entirely. He probably beat her up and told her that was love as well."

They all look at Daphne but she's not telling.

"Well, what is love then?" Rosemary asks.

"You tell us," suggests Daphne, "since you're the one so besotted at the moment."

"Are you?" Penelope smiles at Rosemary, feeling the conversation take an interesting turn at last.

"Been there, done that," says Bruce. "Hate love," he adds as he falls face down in his salad, "love hate." He crawls across to a couch where he settles down to sleep. The cats follow and curl on his chest. As far as they can tell, in their neat and neutered furriness, being any gender is a drag.

•

It sounds like possums on the roof but really it's Rupert's toe-nails scrambling and scraping the headboard of the ME and YOU bed while Floryan screams inside himself "What am I doing, what am I doing what the fuckfuckfuck am I doing?" though he knows very well what it is he's doing, it's the why of it he doesn't understand.

Next morning, Rupert having obligingly crept away so they didn't have to face each other, Floryan understands his actions perfectly. He'd done it because it was there. Because he could. Because his first bloody sentence was no bloody good. He wishes he hadn't. He'd thought he was over having sex for sex's sake, just because he could, because it was there. He was bored with himself. Maybe he'd become celibate. He has one friend who'd decided to and stuck to it and felt better about his life, or so he said. Trouble is, if he did that, he might become even more bored with himself than he is now because sex does fill in a bit of time and it is interesting. Even bad sex is interesting in its own way. There were the unexpected smells and tastes, twists and turns, the overcome revulsions that must be good for the soul—practically a charity you could say, answering all those wants and needs, or were those two last things the same thing? Better to want than to need, thinks Floryan. It doesn't seem so urgent.

There's a cat round here somewhere. Floryan supposes it goes with the house. It's a lonely, scatty sort of cat with bald patches above its eyes, and no one has bothered to tell Floryan its name. Floryan takes out roast chicken left over from the night before last and gives it to the cat, which comes running the second the fridge door opens. While he's about it, Floryan tears a piece off for himself and moves to the window, chewing, resigning himself to another day in the fish tank fussing over his grandmother's cunt. Perhaps he should go on and finish the book and then reconsider this sentence or perhaps he should do the gentlemanly thing and leave his poor old gran out of it entirely or perhaps he should walk into Katoomba in search of a proper cup of coffee.

Of course he's forgotten about Daphne but here she is, cycling purposefully up the drive before the bike slides sideways on a drift of loose gravel, and Floryan hurries to the aid of his fellow writer.

·

At last she's finished *The Witching Hour*. It has taken her most of the night. All the while huge moths with horns and devils' faces bashed at the outside of the house, crashed through windows, stunned themselves against the bedside light. Rosemary picks up her watch from among the corpses on the bedside table. She remembers the neat travel alarm she'd lost in Bali. She keeps meaning to replace it.

The house is very quiet. Daphne, no doubt, has already gone out in search of bodies. Rosemary stays where she is, watching the gently moving tops of trees and a few soft clouds, which is all you can see from the windows in this room, giving it a sense of flight and freedom. Rosemary thinks more about Bali. She'd taken Marie with her, hoping that a holiday might distract her friend from her sadness over the recent death of her partner, Georgina. It hadn't worked. The beauty of Bali had withered in the face of Marie's intractable grief and Rosemary hadn't dealt with it very well, or so she had thought, but then, when she'd thought about it again afterward she doubted anyone could have coped with those drunken nights of insistence that had Georgie lived she would have been the greatest country and western singer Australia had ever produced—a claim Rosemary found difficult to grasp and almost impossible to discuss seriously. And then at a fire dance Marie had sustained a nasty burn on her thin ankle that rapidly turned into a seeping crater. Faced twice daily with the task of cleansing and dressing a wound that she could not help but see as nothing more than an oozing metaphor for deep-dug grief, Rosemary had suggested they cut the holiday short and so they'd come home four days early.

Rosemary had seen Marie recently, having lunch in the sushi bar at the fish market with her new lover, Caroline, a round woman, pink as the new skin that had eventually grown over the old wound.

A helicopter flies low over the house and back again. Rosemary stays snug where she is, thinking of war and rescue and people who find themselves in trouble on narrow ledges as a result of their leisure activities and hectic ideas of fun, and of course she thinks of Billie too, in bed beside her—if only—in this tree house of a room, which causes her to turn her mind to soft and surely sensible places far removed from rocky outcrops, impossible terrain, and jumping from high places with only a string tied round the ankle standing between you and death.

While she thinks on these things Bruce crawls about in the undergrowth beneath her window admiring his dope plants. They're so close to being ready it makes him dribble—but no, wait, the fucking helicopter's back again, lower and slower, taking another run over the target, Bruce thinks, and now as the windows start to rattle Rosemary decides to get up.

She goes to the phone and orders her mushroom compost and the Dynamic Lifter, then she goes to the window and sees the feathery plant tops quiver as Bruce bolts from the garden bed and jumps up onto the verandah. Rosemary walks through to the kitchen and puts the kettle on. It's quieter now. The chopper's switched direction and is going away, but Bruce isn't convinced they've gone.

"Every year," he moans, "just when it's nearly ready to harvest, the bastards come over. How do they know?"

"Perhaps they don't," suggests Rosemary. "Perhaps they're just looking for a lost child or an escaped prisoner."

"They might be, they might," sighs Bruce, scrambling through his pockets until he finds what he needs and, with trembling fingers, fixes a joint.

"Here's to paranoia, man," he mocks himself as he passes it to Rosemary.

．

Floryan, wearing thin rubber gloves, dabs at the gravel rash on Daphne's knee with a piece of damp cotton wool held by tweezers. He'd been dying for a chance to use the first-aid box with the big red cross on it that sits on the shelf in the downstairs bathroom and he'd been dying to use the gloves, too. He'd almost suggested it last night but hadn't wanted Rupert flouncing off in a huff.

They are in the long sitting room where there are a lot of cheap ugly bookcases filled with dead Australian books donated, it looks like, in large job lots by publishers. Some are sideways and some are upside down, covers curling in the sun. On his first night here Floryan used a few to get the fire going but they hadn't worked, just smouldered darkly for hours, leaving a residue of sticky black ash.

Daphne sits on a large purple vinyl chair that, surely, could never have been Edith's. Floryan kneels in front of her with a bowl of warm water to dip his swab in. She looks down at the top of Floryan's head and the neat parting plowed into dark hair dense as a doormat that she wants to reach out and touch and then, possibly, to kiss. Daphne, knowing the impulse to be a natural response to the unfamiliar pleasantness of being taken care of, saves them both difficulty by blinking the thought away, concentrating instead on the plastic curve of his right ear through which the sun shines, highlighting a purple-rimmed area of a bony denture pink riddled with rivulets fed by impossibly intricate tributaries of bright blood, and so the impulse passes. Somewhere, at the back of the house, a door slams.

"Dot," says Floryan, applying an antiseptic cream. "She'll make us coffee and then she can show you the garden. I know nothing about it but the garden was a big part of the whole thing, you know. Dot was a girl at the time and worshipped Mrs. Black. When the town turned against the family, the stalwart Dot stood by her, though I don't think she cared much for the others." And then, getting to his feet, "They should do something about that gravel. They put too much down in the first place. . . . What's that?"

Floryan and Daphne move to the French windows. The helicopter slices through a cloud and swoops sideways. Trees chatter and grind together like teeth. A figure runs across the lawn and vanishes into the dark clasp of the camellias.

"Who was that?"

"The secateurs murderer," states Daphne with absolute certainty.

"Ooh! Do you think?" Floryan's afraid she might insist on giving chase but she doesn't.

·

Rosemary and Bruce are running about because the struggle is over and paranoia has won. It's all very well tearing the plants out of the ground but then what? All thirty-five of them piled under the old pine trees behind the house. *Thirty-five.* How can she not have noticed? She remembers some talk of two or three but what on earth would the penalty for so many be? Bruce doesn't know. He sticks to the point of view that it is better to be hung for a sheep than for a lamb. Rosemary doesn't want to be hung for anything, nor does she wish to be fined, imprisoned, lose her job, or be in any way publicized or inconvenienced. She is therefore desperate to get all this greenery off her property. The throb of the returning helicopter increases her resolve. They must take it somewhere else quickly. Preceded by its thrashing shadow, the helicopter moves slowly above them.

"Piss off. Bastards. Now I know what it was like to be those what were they? Black pajamas, cone-shaped hats, little rubber thongs?"

"Vietcong." Rosemary's trying to think of the straightest person she knows so they can go there and, until things cool off, hide the dope somewhere on this person's property. Attics, basements, garden sheds; the atmosphere, the likely furniture of such places dance briefly in her head. It's quiet now, just a police siren wailing from the direction of the highway.

"We should boil some water and scald the stems. It seals in the resin, apparently." Rosemary ignores this information. She simply doesn't wish to know. She feels grown-up and remote from such concerns, which, given her age, is possibly not surprising; it is even, as she tells herself sternly, about time. Bruce feels no such restriction.

"Come and get me, copper," he screams at the retreating helicopter. "I bet they've radioed the fuzz in that car. I bet they're on the way to bust us." But the coast seems to be clearing if not yet clear. The siren is fading into the distance and the helicopter isn't coming back. Bruce sits groaning and grieving beside his ragged crop. He can't take it home. It makes Penelope cross. She wasn't always like that but she is now. She's not averse to a snort or puff of whatever's going, it's just she's not as keen on it as she was and she's certainly not eager to take risks for it. Bruce observes increased caution in all his friends. They wrap it round them to keep out trouble. And a fat lot of good it will do them. He treasures the few remaining diehards, despite Penelope's increasing efforts to ban them from the house.

"It can't stay here, you know. It'll have to go." He should've known. He did know. At least he's not surprised.

"All right. I understand."

Bruce sets about stripping the stalks and leaves from the plants and stuffing them into the old duvet cover she's provided. He shoves it into the trunk of Rosemary's car while she goes inside to put on something more substantial than the worn pink cotton pajamas she's been trotting round the garden in. She pulls on the black leather R.M. Williams boots she bought yesterday and as she does this the thought streaks in from somewhere so fast there's no time to duck that these boots will last longer than she will. There are times when Rosemary feels about as equipped to deal with the world as does the average chimpanzee. She starts to cry until she remembers that these days even a two-minute weep leaves her puffed and soggy as a three-day-old corpse fished from the ocean. She finishes dressing, puts on a bit of make-up to disguise tear damage, and goes out to deal with what she can deal with and forget about what she can't. She chops up the bare woody stems with a spade and carts them to the compost heap. She rakes the so-called lawn clear of all traces. The garden beds have a cratered look. Rosemary thinks she'll put in some roses, which are legal and pretty. Yes. Rosemary feels better. She feels like a drink. They drive to Bruce's shop where he tapes a note to the door that reads "closed due to ill health" and then they drive to the pub, passing the church, which has a sign outside that says BLESSED ARE THEY THAT MOVE IN STRAIGHT CIRCLES, which Rosemary has to stop and take a picture of.

In the pub Bruce starts to talk about his mother.

"One thing she told me I've never forgotten," he confides.

"Only one?" Rosemary wishes she had been so fortunate.

"She said always to remember cats are human too."

They drink three whiskies and start to feel a lot better about everything. Bruce is inclined to be sanguine about his spoiled crop. Next year will be different. They can send in the marines if they like but he'll hang tough.

"They still haven't got that bloke," says the barman.

"What bloke's that?"

"The one who chops off ladies' fingers. He struck again last night. Then some kids reckon they spotted this bloke with blood all over him walking along the railway line just this side of Mount Victoria so the cops sent up a chopper to search the area. Reckon he'll be miles away by now."

Well, not quite, though he soon will be as he tiptoes past Rosemary's car and sees keys that have fallen from her pocket. Great. Nice car. He thinks he'll go over to Perth to see his brother who's bound to see him right, though what he'll do for gas on what is, after all, a very long way is anybody's guess.

.

Dot dashes across the grass beside the dry stone wall. She holds a rock tied to a length of string tied to the tendril of a climbing rose. She skids to a stop, windmills her arm, releases the stone, and watches with a crow of pleasure as it sails neatly over the wall. Dot turns to Daphne.

"See. That's how she used to do it. Then you just go round the other side, untie the string, and Bob's your uncle you've got your rose growing up over the wall." Was there no end to Edith Black's ingenuity? Daphne takes a picture of the wall, the stone, and the rose with her Polaroid camera and thanks Dot. Daphne bought the camera first thing this morning intending to use it rather than the pencil sketches she's been doing until now. It's quicker, obviously, and she likes the sound of it, the urgent hiss and spit.

"You sure there's nothing else? Like the woodpile?"

"Woodpile?"

"She had such a way with a woodpile, Mrs. Black. She bought this book about them. Each country has different methods of stacking firewood, you see. All different shapes and patterns. She was working her way through them all. Very pretty, most of them were. I remember her doing it over several winters. She'd prop the book up on a log, put on her gloves, and stack up the wood just like in the picture."

Dot has led Daphne to a dank area of the garden under two large cedar trees where wood is stacked in a quite unremarkable way. "Well, you can imagine," says Dot, and indeed Daphne can. She sees Edith, gaunt she remembers, thin for sure, snowflakes clinging briefly to the salt and pepper fringe protruding from the tightly tied headscarf of pure Australian wool, paisley patterned, her thin legs in boots of dark brown suede with a warm woolly lining, scissoring back and forth in the gathering dark, and as she watches her eyes fill and the figure wavers and what she's left with, apart from Dot capering in front of her face, is a head-to-toe tingle, like a quick frisk with a razor blade, which tells her her mother is present and trying to tell her something—that what she intends to do is not enough, probably, since nothing was ever enough for Isobel. And it doesn't seem like much in the face of the lonely unflinching gallantry of Daphne's subjects, her mother's generation with their dumb diaries, their scorched lamb chops, their dull exiles, the intermittently rewarding office jobs, their wifedom and their love or lack of it, their darkness housed in umbrella cupboards, their committee memberships, typing of minutes, writing of letters, their cats, dogs, and ailing parents, all this and also, yes, in some cases the smattering of importunate but rewarding—or so they insist—children, which of course, in Isobel's case, included Daphne. And if this wasn't enough there was also the question of their adherence to various codes of behavior, the claws of their consciences lodged deep in the scaly sides of the boring blunted dinosaur of literary nationalism, and, worse yet, Communism as it blundered through their lives and times.

"Smile please," cries Dot, grabbing the camera and taking Daphne's picture as she stands uncertain beneath the trees with Isobel's blood thumping through her veins, howling, sobbing, grinding its teeth.

"I love these things," says Dot, watching Daphne's image swim to the surface of the square of cardboard she holds in her hand. "Like they say, a picture's worth a thousand words, isn't that it?"

Yes, that *is* it. Exactly. Precisely. Pictures. And now Daphne has it. It will all be recorded on live flesh, her flesh, in pictures with blood running through them. Will that do? She hopes so. It seems the perfect method of record for these intermingled lives involving, as it must, a bit of pain and a lot of mockery.

"Thank you, Dot," says Daphne. "You've been a great help."

All she needs now is someone who is imaginative, talented, and hygienic to help her do what she must. Then at last she notices the small inky butterfly fluttering sweetly on Dot's cheekbone. How could she not have seen? What other graphics are dotted round Dot? Daphne wants to tear the woman's clothes off instantly and find out but decides to ask a few questions instead. Yes, there are other designs and, once they're indoors out of the cold, she'll be happy to show them to Daphne. They were all done by her daughter, who has gone to America to study her craft further but her time's up so she'll be back soon. If not this week then certainly next, Dot thinks, and she's also willing to bet she'll come straight home because the girl's bound to have spent all the money she has in the world and then some.

"She's a fully paid up member of the QEWU," adds Dot proudly.

"QEWU?"

"Queer and Esoteric Workers' Union."

Daphne writes down Dot's phone number, mounts her bike. As she prepares to ride away, Dot grabs her arm.

"Mrs. Black was the last one to see your poor mum alive, you know. They'd had a falling out, you see. About the telephone, it was. Doctor Black was always very particular that the phone be answered. Not by me, mind. He didn't trust a Koori to get a message straight. No, Mrs. Black had to do it. It interrupted her work, and no mistake. Anyhow, this particular day she was talking to your mum. Very deep in conversation, they were, when the blessed phone rings. Well. 'Don't answer the bloody thing,' says Isobel. 'But I must,' cries poor Mrs. Black. 'Oh, no, you mustn't. What we're talking about is important and if you answer that phone the point will be lost,' yelps your mum and quick as a flash she was across the room and ripping the phone out of the wall. Well, I'd never seen anything like it. Neither had Mrs. Black so she asks your mother to leave and she did. Mrs. Black felt very bad about it afterward, when she heard what happened next. But you'd have to say she was provoked. Especially later, when she found the nasty spider your mum had put in her bed before she left."

Daphne decides not to inquire into this spider business. She'll save it for another day. She has this vision of the provoking Isobel creeping bedraggledly away, banished from the doorstep because, unlike those who believed so much, Isobel believed in nothing at all—except, that is, her talent.

·

A police car, Rosemary inside it, pulls up outside the house. The nursery has delivered the mushroom compost while she was out, leaving it in the wrong place, of course. Rosemary sits staring at the stuff piled in front of her garage doors wondering why anyone would leave it there. Also thinking: Even if my car hadn't been stolen I couldn't put it away. And then: If people separate, go their different ways, what happens? Herself and Billie. Like railway lines laid in a desert, flat black tracks racing away across red soil never to meet again. Except they do seem to meet in the farthest distance at the edge of the world, but the point recedes as you go toward it. Rosemary wants to leave, now. Hire a car and chase Billie. Throw herself across the tracks. Cling dizzily to the spinning edge of the world. Stop the process of separation. She could take Bruce along for company, though what she'd do with him when they got there she couldn't say.

The cop, seeing she's off with the fairies and not about to get out of his car, does so himself. He walks round and opens the passenger door. He clears his throat.

"Don't worry. It's in our hands now, love." Rosemary stares at his hands. No car there. Her mind immediately begins to list those things, dear to her, she wouldn't ever want to see in those hands. She drags this thought, growling, away.

"I'd get in touch with my insurance people right away if I was you."

Rosemary nods and gets out of the car. She feels exhausted. She also feels a familiar stickiness between her legs that explains why she feels the way she's been feeling lately and why she dropped her car keys. How unfair. With so little time left she didn't want to spend any of it bleeding and losing keys and the like. As the witching hour approaches, she sees it could have its advantages.

Sergeant MacAlpine's having a good look round the garden. At least, thinks Rosemary, he's not younger than me. He is, actually; he just looks old and awful.

"It's the shock, I should think," he tells her, perhaps to explain her lack of anything to say. "It's no good, losing a car. It's an expensive thing. And then there's the contents. You must make a list while it's all fresh in your mind. You can claim it."

Rosemary supposes this is true. She hasn't had time to think about it yet. She doesn't want to, either. Do insurance companies actually pay up? Rosemary's never quite believed it. What had been in the car, anyway? She's not sure. Her camera, of course, because she'd just used it, a dozen tapes. A jacket? Not her leather one, she hopes. She remembers now, can see her favorite jacket chucked on the backseat. Oh fuck. The dope, in the trunk. Rosemary laughs, which at least gets rid of the sergeant who, having run out of advice and detecting hysteria, eases himself back into his car, frowns, takes the heavily fingermarked mirrored sunglasses he keeps on the dash and wraps them carefully round his sweaty head, raises a hand in fat salute, and drives away, leaving the ungrateful bitch to sort it out for herself.

.

*D*aphne lights a cigarette, approximately her seventy-third today. Daphne's determined to enjoy as many smokes as she can in this life because she's fairly certain there'll be none in the next.

"But doesn't it make you feel ill?" cries Rosemary, menstrual, sensitive, brooding on the almost certain loss of her leather jacket.

"No. It makes me feel better," insists Daphne, "much better." She squints through smoke at the day's crop of Polaroids pinned to the wall in the spare room. Dot, grinning, capers across the balding lawn clutching her rose-throwing equipment. The rest are of derelict houses, some not much more than uncertain oblongs, marked by bits of brick sticking out of the ground, middens of broken bottles and jagged rusty cans.

Daphne hopes Rosemary won't start talking about nicotine patches or chewing gum and she doesn't. Obviously the loss of her car distracts her. Rosemary's told her about it. Awful. Bad luck. Poor thing. Have a cigarette. No, no, sorry, course not. Have a drink.

Daphne wants to talk about what she's doing because she's feeling excited about it. She won't, though, not yet. She'll wait until Rosemary's mood improves. It does seem to be, slowly. At least she's starting to think about dinner, which is a good sign, surely. Some people are coming and there's no food and nothing to go and get it in, so Daphne obligingly hooks a string bag to her handlebars and cycles off to fetch a chicken and a few other things Rosemary will need to throw together a green chicken curry, and of course some tampons because Rosemary's run out.

·

At the exit leading to a dull and scruffy mining town well west of the mountains, Rosemary's car, low on gas, leaves the highway. The pressing question is how to obtain gas without paying for it. As it happens, it's simple. The driver fills the car and drives away fast. The service station manager runs outside, too late. The car's a dark blur up the road. She hasn't a hope of getting the number. The owner hasn't the cash to put in a security camera and, besides, the place is so small. Oh well. She won't say anything and see if he notices. Basically, she doesn't think he will, he's such a moron. She hopes he won't. He'd certainly blame her and take it out of her wages or even give her the sack and she really needs this job since her mum was laid off.

"Go for it," she yells after the offending car. She wishes she were in it with him, whoever he is. But then he'd probably want to fuck her for the privilege of his company so forget it. Save up, girl, she tells herself, then you can do what you like when you like with who you like. Something flies, batlike, from the window of the fleeing car. She runs up the road to see. A leather jacket lies in the dust. She puts it on over her ripped jeans and T-shirt. It's fantastic.

·

*C*hopping the chicken into manageable portions, Rosemary tries to organize her life in similar fashion. In the morning she will work. In the afternoon she will garden. In the evenings she will do whatever comes along and if nothing does she will watch television. She might vary things a bit by going for a walk or healing the sick. "Amen," she says.

Above the spit and sputter of browning chicken the day's news drones along on the television. Transferring the chicken pieces to squares of paper towel, she hears what it is Daphne's saying to the television in the next room.

"The brutes. Who are these people, what are these people, and why are they doing these things?" as on the screen a man, dying of AIDS, stares at her from some distant inner chamber of hell where refugees, fleeing those of their fellow countrymen who wish to cut them into pieces, have stolen the mattress from under him.

"A moving tide of humanity streaming across the border,"

intones the reporter, though Daphne doubts the human part, but then what other creature on the planet behaves like this, wonders Daphne as she watches a gang of young men beat those smaller than themselves on the head to gain possession of a bag of biscuits. This looks like humanity all right. "I mean, can't their mothers do something about them? And I don't think postcolonial stress syndrome is sufficient explanation."

"Oh shit," cries Rosemary from the doorway, "they're vegetarians."

"I don't think so. And anyway, I can't see that that is any excuse either," says Daphne.

"Not them. Jim and his wife. I forgot. How could I do that? What can I do? There's nothing here and they'll be here any minute, they're always on time." And so it is that Daphne, having first phoned the local Indian restaurant to order ahead, finds herself saddling up her bike again and pedaling off into the night. Rosemary opens the windows and flaps about to get rid of meaty cooking smells and puts the curry in the fridge for tomorrow.

•

Rupert gives Marcus his nightly veggieburger and decides to take him for a walk. Rupert's a Buddhist and so is his dog. The closest Marcus ever gets to a bone is a corn cob. Marcus is terribly pleased to be going somewhere although at the end of the lead he can tell his master is anxious. That's because they are on their way to do a deal, with any luck, at the local French restaurant.

"No dogs are allowed," squeals Madame, but they ignore her and walk through the dining room crammed with couples and bus parties. Marcus, driven off his head by meaty smells, trails long ropes of slobber. In the kitchen they find Pierre, who, all main courses being cooked and out, is smoking a ciga-rillo and watching a video on a screen mercifully obscured, at least from Rupert's point of view, by steam rising from the *bain-marie*. There's no sound as two men and one woman who looks terribly young do extreme things together on a mattress on a floor in a cheap room somewhere.

"Deesgusteeng," says Pierre. "But she likes eeet, you know." He means Madame, which is a lie. "On beezy nights it take 'er mind off all thees bloody food which she 'ates and so do I. I 'eard you 'ad geeven it up, no?"

"No," says Rupert firmly.

"I 'eard you got up one night and flushed your stash down ze toilet."

"Not me, old son."

"Well, there's nutting 'ere. I 'ave to order in for you, special. For which a deposeet ees required, as you know, no?"

"Yes, yes." Rupert hands over the hundred-dollar note he's brought for this purpose. "When?"

"Oh, day aftair tomorrow or ze day aftair zat."

"I'll be back," promises Rupert, and they leave.

"I 'ate zis dirty 'abit," calls Madame as they pass, which is rich to say the least, in Rupert's opinion. What else does she think keeps this dump running?

Walking homeward down the mall Rupert sees lights in the

kitchen behind the deli run by his friend Roy. He also sees
Daphne approaching on her bike and waves. She stops and asks
him to dinner, thinking an extra vegetarian one way or the
other won't make much difference. Rupert says he'd love to,
he'll be along in a minute. The thing is, the lights at the back
of the deli have reminded Rupert of the fact that a friend of
Roy's does deals a lot cheaper than Pierre. It's a pity he didn't
remember it earlier. It was just such a fear of short-term
memory loss that had caused him to leap up in the middle of
the night and flush his stash down the toilet. But it could be
put down to age, surely? After all, he is sixty-three and can
hardly be expected to remember every last detail of the trivia
surrounding him. Like how old his mother is, the wicked
green creature. Anyway, she's not too clear about it either. It
didn't seem right to still have a mother at his age, never mind
worrying about her. Now the main thing is to get the cash
back. Luckily, he too has watched the refugees in the news this
evening and now they provide him with an idea. He marches
back to the restaurant, remembers Madame, veers round the
back because, after all, he doesn't want to upset anyone any
more than he is about to. He instructs Marcus to sit and enters
the kitchen. No use beating about the bush so Rupert comes
straight to the point. He can see the corner of his hundred-
dollar bill poking from Pierre's white chef's jacket. If push
comes to shove, he'll grab it and run.

"Sorry, old love, but I've made a bit of a miscalculation."

"Oh?" Pierre folds his arms across his chest to protect the
cash. Never mind. Rupert can set Marcus on him if necessary.

"Yes. I thought I had two. But I didn't."

"Two?"

"I thought so, yes. Two hundred. But really I only had one. And that particular one was targeted for a better cause. So I want it back."

"What better cause?"

"Where've you been, old love? It's for those refugees."

"What refugees?"

"The ones on the TV." Panic. The truth is, he can't remember *which*. Aren't they all much the same? Why is he putting himself through this to get something that's ruining his mind? On the other hand, who can keep track? Who'd want to? It's one thing after another, and often several things at once. He remembers the Gulf War, though. They'd interrupted the late night reruns of *Prisoner: Cell Block H* to show the war live and forgot to put it back when it was won. Things like that you don't forget, thinks Rupert, growing terse.

"Look, I want my money back. That's all."

"Why didn't you say so?" Pierre twitches the hundred-dollar bill from his pocket and holds it out to Rupert.

"I bloody well did, mate." Rupert snatches at the money. Pierre moves it slightly and Rupert misses. Pierre leans toward him and tucks it into the pocket of Rupert's jeans jacket. He pats his shoulder and steers him to the back door, through it, and out onto the street.

"You don't sound like a bloody Frog to me, mate," cries Rupert at the closing door. "Well, he doesn't, does he?" Marcus whines sympathetically. "Anyway, I was firm and I got our money back, old son." Marcus thumps his tail on the pavement. The sound of one dog clapping. They cross the road to the deli and tap on the glass of the darkened shop.

.

*L*ater, in bed after what was undoubtedly a successful evening because everyone enjoyed themselves including herself, Rosemary, prodded along by the bits of horrid news she'd seen on television earlier in the evening, takes herself on her own punishing walk along a length of gray-green greasy water that is not the Limpopo—though there are connections—but rather the River Thames near Oxford.

There was a time when she walked this path in her thoughts nearly every night but then the months had stacked up and toppled, sliding over into twenty-seven years of separation from Sapphire and her baby Shirley until—disappointingly because she'd sworn in her case it wouldn't—time had cured all things, or most of them. But still she wants to know where they are. They could be nowhere because they could be dead. They could be trapped in one of those vexed Third World venues where the Four Horsemen of the Apocalypse have gone to ground. Or more likely Sapphire is still running the small mixed business in the Oxford back street where Rosemary first found her.

She'd gone into this shop for the first time to buy cigarettes, the machine at the pub being broken. After that she'd been back again and again—Mars bars, baked beans, salt and vinegar crisps, pints of milk—all bought from the gorgeous woman behind the counter. From behind a bead curtain at the back of the shop, the roar of males watching sporting events on television could be heard. Until, reckless, "Will you come out and have a drink with me one night?"

"I don't drink alcohol."

"Tea."

"I may not leave my house at night." That's what you think, thought Rosemary, proposing a daytime time, a date for the drinking of tea. Sapphire agreed and the thing's begun, leading to the moment when Rosemary, living in hope and fueled by fantasy, placed the longest ladder she could carry against the dark brick wall of the shop. Rosemary encouraged Sapphire over the windowsill of the back bedroom while her husband and his two brothers played cards in the front one. That baby Shirley would be lowered first into her grasping hands she hadn't bargained for. Had not, even, considered, which surprises her now since you'd hardly leave a girl behind in the charge of that lot.

The houseboat and in the dark, a darker secret. She hadn't heard of female circumcision. How could she take pleasure in anything so pleasureless? Sapphire refused to comfort her, no reason why she should but "at least," whined Rosemary, wounded, "you could have told me."

"What words would I have to do that?" inquired Sapphire.

Bitter Rosemary, selfish, sad, hunched on a bollard, trying to light a Silk Cut in the endless fucking wind off the water, ear tips turning blue before some blunt instrument landed between those cold ears and fade out fade in, she'd opened her eyes on an empty morning, gray, the rotten vegetable smell of the Thames catching at the back of her throat. Winter trees clawed the sky. An empty scotch bottle, one of those big ones people buy at duty-free shops, rolled away under her foot.

She'd gone below to find toys, clothing, the remains of last night's supper smeared, for some reason, over walls and portholes, dishes smashed and Sapphire gone. Sapphire with her girl child and her weight of scars. Sapphire tracked down, cornered in the night, reclaimed by those she'd tried so hard to escape. How could she and Rosemary have expected otherwise? How could they have attempted to make a life in the teeth of such a storm?

Her world reduced to irregular bits she couldn't piece together, Rosemary had stood in a maze of tire tracks on the tow path. In the intact world two schoolgirls trotted by with hockey sticks, short skirts, meaty legs marbled pink with cold. "It must be freezing living on those houseboats," remarked one as they passed.

She'd walked away. She'd not looked back but had walked at a brisk pace back the way she'd come, a return journey made alone. No Sapphire with her plastic bags of belongings and no frightened baby Shirley, bellowing as her stroller reeled through ruts across the muddy bank, charged at by hissing geese, her head, bruised by the icy wind, sprouting a purple and plum-like bloom.

Rosemary had kept on walking until she reached her former life, her room at college, her books, possessions, interrupted PhD, letters waiting from her family back home to which she'd replied providing no explanation for her silence and receiving no request for one in return. They trusted her. It made her cry that they should love her so much and that nobody loved Sapphire though many wanted her for various reasons having to do with them and not with Sapphire and among that number, Rosemary had to admit, was Rosemary.

Rosemary adjusts her pillows and tries to do the same for her memories. You can tell yourself differing versions of this and that until the truth, which was never all that truthful to begin with, is softened and molded into the most comfortable version of events. What had she honestly wanted? To rescue Sapphire from her arranged marriage full of pain and shop work. To lead her back to Australia on a lead attached to a silver-studded black leather collar and to keep baby Shirley tucked in a basket at the foot of their bed while an awful lot of fucking went on?

Rosemary tries to work out how much she's drunk tonight. Too much obviously. Lonely and pissed, she thinks.

"Lonely and pissed," she says out loud and is answered by banging on the front door. How Daphne can sleep through it is a mystery but she does. She must take pills.

Alan stands shivering on the doorstep, face pale, eyes red, nose as well. He's sick, too sick to drive back to town in his new car from wherever it is he's been. It's the flu, he thinks.

Everyone in the department has got this bloody flu and now he's coming down with it too.

Rosemary puts a match to the fire laid ready in the grate because you never know in the mountains when you'll need one and makes tea with honey and lemon and a good shot of whisky. Hearing Alan sneezing she decides to create a line of defense and makes herself one too. I drink too much, thinks Rosemary. She fetches wood from the box on the verandah and builds up the fire. Perhaps I drink too much sometimes, she amends.

"You seem very pleased to see me," observes Alan suspiciously.

"I am," says Rosemary, but offers no explanation. "Daphne's in the spare room, but we can make you up a bed on the sofa out here. I'll find you a nightie."

"Thanks. Just as long as it's exactly the same as yours. What are those creatures cavorting all over it?" He plucks at her flanneletted arm. "Long-nosed mice in nightcaps or are they elephants? I know, it's Babar. I want one too. Got a thermometer? Got any aspirin? Got any good books? So now, sweetest, tell me. What is it exactly Daphne's up to?"

Now there's a good question. Whatever it is, she's not losing any sleep over it.

•

Daphne finds the ruined house in Blackheath she cannot find by day. It is, she is certain, the scene of her mother's auto-da-fé. Daphne sprays the outline of a body sprawled on the ground.

The dark bar of shadow cast by the old chimney falls across it like an accusing finger. Daphne takes a picture. She walks back to her bike. Mounts. Dismounts, lets it topple down to lie in the dirt. She walks back to the white outline she has made and lies down, fitting herself neatly inside it. Brushing away a few ants and pebbles she rests her cheek gently on the ground. It doesn't look comfortable but it is and, more than that, it is comforting and comforted, Daphne wakes to the murmuring of voices in the sitting room.

.

The car thief is doing okay, proceeding quietly in a westerly direction. He'd filled up again in Cobar, using the same method, and has made it to Broken Hill. Can he get away with it again? He does. He feels gentle, expansive, tentatively benign as he pulls off the road in a cloud of red dust and pees on a patch of prickly pear.

Back in the car he sucks thoughtfully on a strand of pasta from the packet he found on the floor in the back of the car. It must've slipped out of a plastic bag on the way home from Kmart the other night. It's kept him going, anyway. He's gone into shops and asked for glasses of water and never been refused. At least two people have made him cups of tea and all have provided biscuits. He looks forward to Perth, to the prosperous suburb in which, he believes, his younger brother lives. He hasn't seen this brother for a long time though he wrote him a letter from jail once and received a swift and brief reply that referred unkindly, among other things, to the event that occurred on the day our murderer left home, an event he'd more or less forgotten and wasn't too keen to think about even now. All in all the letter wasn't that encouraging but most likely, when they're face to face yarning over a beer or two—he can see it, just the two of them, on a distant verandah at dusk, the light dying on the Swan River—they will clear the air, shake hands, hug.

•

Encouraged by Alan from a pleasingly dappled spot on the side verandah, Rosemary works in her garden. She moves all the compost, mulches, plants, waters, trims, and enjoys herself. Alan, feeling better, moves himself into the hammock strung between the two big fir trees where he dozes and reads and cuddles Kristeva when she'll let him. He shows no sign of leaving. Rosemary's glad—for one thing she has the use of his car in which to transport her new rosebushes and, for another, she likes to be encouraged even if it's only in the simple matter of choosing the spot to hang a seed cone for the birds.

Using Alan's laptop she finishes her book reviews and faxes them through in good time. At breakfast, Alan flicks through one of the books in question, frowns at the author's photograph.

"She was born in 1973," he complains.

"I don't think we can hold that against her."

"I don't see why not."

"Try this jam," suggests Rosemary, spreading a generous

amount on her own piece of toast. She examines the label. "It says it's homemade."

"Yes. But whose home?"

Rosemary picks up a copy of the *Blue Mountains Gazette* because she intends to take advantage of the low summer rates by ordering a load of ironbark from one of the wood merchants who advertise in this paper.

When this wood is delivered Alan and Rosemary stack it. They are sunk in self-congratulatory beers on the verandah when Daphne comes home. They direct frothy smiles in the direction of their handiwork. Daphne inspects. Daphne sighs.

"Australians haven't a clue how to stack wood," she says and, without so much as a by-your-leave, begins deconstructing their woodpile. She hurls pieces in four directions, roughly according to size apparently. When it's scattered all over the grass, she walks away.

"I'll finish it in the morning," she tells them.

"Fair enough," says Rosemary, though God knows why. It's one of those things that slips out when all else fails.

"She *is* a funny girl," says Alan.

.

Alone in bed at night Rosemary wants to make love. She reflects on the amount of time she's spent tossed about the landscape by desire. Passion lavished on this person and that which, entertaining though it had been, she now thinks she could have directed into other things. On the other hand, what other things? Not much could rival the enthrallment of those high dyke dramas, the lacerating crystal kisses, the turmoil, tangled sheets, midnight flights and moonlit drives, paradise by the dashboard light all laid down on a soundtrack; popular music, the great fixative of emotion. At the end of the affair cassettes flew from the car window. The letters, the photos, the fringed suede jacket she bought you in Mexico twenty-three years ago, the fashion, the letters, and in more recent times the faxes forming a tidemark of litter at the outer edges of her life. Perhaps she should have put her spare time to worthier use, eliminating illiteracy, repairing all main roads.

Kristeva jumps onto the bed. Rosemary strokes her cat but who will stroke Rosemary? Should she go out and find a wife to grow old with?

The headachy smell of a mosquito coil drifts in. Rosemary's fingers find a flea in the fur under Kristeva's collar and squish it.

"Poor old pussy," she whispers and immediately wishes she hadn't.

Out in the garden Daphne murmurs with Dot's daughter who's come round earlier. They've been sitting at the outside table for three hours now. Every so often their voices rise in a pitch of excitement and then become cautious and muffled again. Daphne, clearly anxious that Rosemary not talk to this young woman too much, ushered her guest off into the garden to talk. Listening to them now, Rosemary thinks how pleasant it is, having people around. She's not sure where Alan's gone tonight. He slipped off after dinner, in tight ripped jeans and leather vest, tossing his keys and merry of step. She supposes

Rupert has provided him with a list of local beats and he's gone to check them out. He may well have lent Alan the clothes too. Rosemary had never seen Alan wear such things before but he probably has closets full of them at home. Rosemary wishes she could stitch on a dick and join him out there in the dark, in the hot rain just starting, driving Daphne and her new mate—her name's Lois, Rosemary now remembers—indoors and straight to the liquor cupboard and thence to the door of Rosemary's bedroom where they stand grinning, girlish, clutching three fat brandy glasses and a bottle of cognac, clearly keen on celebrating something. What is this, is everyone out there scoring tonight except her?

"Here's to hybridism," toasts Daphne. "If that's the word."

Rosemary has no idea what this means, and clearly neither of them is going to supply an explanation, but she drinks to it anyway.

.

Next morning, in the butcher's, where they have gone to buy meat for Kristeva, Daphne decides to tell Rosemary of her plans. Rosemary is purchasing two lamb's kidneys, one heart, and a handful of the best ground beef when Daphne blurts it out.

"Eat here or take away?" inquires Wayne the butcher.

Stung by Wayne's witticism, Rosemary barely registers the fact that her friend is proposing to turn herself into a large picture book with some qualifying text. Indeed, she's scarcely listening as they continue down the mall to purchase milk and the *Sydney Morning Herald* because it's Monday and the paper comes with a supplementary guide to the week's television, without which they would be lost. Rosemary also intends to buy five two-dollar instant scratchies or two five-dollar ones. Bruce reckons you've got more chance with the five-dollar ones but Rosemary enjoys the extra excitement of scratching five times instead of just twice.

"Good morning, good morning, good morning," they cry to passersby, as though they've lived here all their lives and know everyone inside out. Rosemary has visions of this summer stretching on forever, of her and Daphne stuck in the here and now and, thrashing round to escape, breaking the membrane separating this space from that and entering the twilight zone where they walk, aged eighty, down the street with an umbrella over their heads to keep off the sun, squabbling about which of them should hold it. Rosemary dresses herself for this future outing in bright white ankle socks and sandals. Her hands are yellowing packets of brittle bones held together by thin white gloves at the end of each arm. Her sparse white hair, through which the pink skin dimly blinks, is kept back from her faded eyes by a headband, and for some reason she can only attribute to senility, she's wearing a skirt and a blouse with a Peter Pan collar. She looks like a dilapidated baby while Daphne, in bright pink tracksuit and running shoes, is a robust, boastful toddler bowling along at her side. Because of course she's won: *she* holds the umbrella.

But now Daphne, dressed in her customary black and who

certainly never wears pink, not yet anyway, is speaking excitedly of color. Tattoos, colorwise, have improved out of sight, apparently. Also, they are no longer limited to bleeding hearts, serpents, thorns and roses. Complex and subtle of design—Daphne uses the example of one of Lois's clients, an Adelaide businesswoman who has Snugglepot and Cuddlepie embroidered on her bottom, to illustrate her point—they can shine forth like the Sistine Chapel and, should time dull them, they too, like the chapel, can be restored.

"Doesn't it hurt?" Rosemary says, the first thing that enters her mind. Well, needles do hurt, don't they, however worthwhile the reason for sticking them in? Rosemary has recently read an article about acupuncture that said even the Chinese, though they believe the procedure to be beneficial, were nonetheless afraid of the pain involved. Daphne, who hoped for a more excited response to her ideas, looks crestfallen and Rosemary is immediately sorry because it is an interesting, indeed an extraordinary, idea. Self-mutilation as biography. A life recorded on a body and not just turned into yet another narrative text fated to be ignored as Daphne's biography of her mother will surely be. Hadn't Foucault described the body as the inscribed surface of events totally imprinted by history or some such?

"Way to go, Foucault," hums Rosemary, linking her arm through her friend's as they swing into the newsagent, where Rosemary goes for the five two-dollar option.

The trouble is, thinks Daphne as she watches Rosemary

make her purchases, that you have to pick your moment for revelation. Just because you're ready to confide doesn't mean that even your closest friends, distracted by life, are automatically ready to listen. Also Rosemary is so irredeemably middle-class she automatically equates tattooing with sailors, prisoners, and self-mutilating teenagers with low self-images. Rosemary, in Daphne's opinion, is far from perfect. How long, for instance, has she been a compulsive gambler? She can't pass a newsagent without dashing in and buying those stupid instant scratchies. She remembers how Rosemary swore that that time at the Hakoah Club was the first time she'd played keno. Beginner's luck, she'd claimed. Now Daphne suspects it wasn't. Daphne's willing to bet she'd been hanging out there for months. Indeed, she half expects Rosemary to go into a scratching frenzy on the spot, but she doesn't. She just slips the things into her jacket, pats the pocket for luck, and puts her arm round Daphne.

"I'll take you out to lunch," she says. "Where would you like to go?"

But Daphne's not so easily won, although she'd like to be. Perhaps giving in would help her backache, almost constant nowadays.

"Can't," she says. "Got a few things to do," and she walks away, offended, down the mall.

Rosemary's sorry. Now she thinks there could be worse fates than spending her dotage with Daphne. What's wrong with two old ladies toddling along together? Where this leaves Billie she's not sure. But, realistically, Rosemary asks herself, gazing in the bookshop window, it's not likely to work for them, is it? And obliterating everything: what is it like to be old? Seriously old, not just middling, like Rosemary. She wants to jump twenty years and find out. It's as though a curtain she never knew existed had parted and then been jerked shut before she had a chance to have a good look.

Rosemary is conscious of things she's never thought about before. Conscious of being middle-aged when all that's left is the second half, the half when bad things happen. And what has she done with the first half? What is there to show for it? A career that often interested her but equally often didn't, which often seemed worthwhile but which too often did not. Articles printed in publications read by the tiny percentage of the population concerned with these matters. The odd bit of good luck here and there and the odd bit of bad. Checks and balances. Credits and debits. All mush of a mushness. She wants to scream out loud, "I have wasted my entire life," but really, there's no call for that and certainly not in the main street of a place proud to be known as a Garden Village that Welcomes Careful Drivers.

"Good morning," says Rosemary to someone who seems to be smiling at her but she's not paying attention because of this cliff she's standing on the edge of inside her head. Second half be buggered. This is the final quarter.

"You coming to the game next Sunday?" inquires the smiling person who is actually Max, the one who's just committed herself to Annie. And the game in question is the Tops versus Bottoms softball game to be held at the oval in North Katoomba this coming Sunday. "You can join in if you like. The Tops could use a bit of muscle." Astonished at hearing herself thus described, Rosemary says she'll be there.

.

"**D**id you know that women born at the beginning of this century had a life expectancy of forty-six years? Just think, darling, we'd both be dead." Penelope pummels the steering wheel for emphasis. "Now isn't that extraordinary?"

"Extraordinary," repeats Rosemary, thinking: well at least it would all be over by now. At least I'd know. Though what she'd know she can't say. Besides, she doesn't believe a word of what Penelope has just said. People are always saying things like that.

Penelope and Rosemary are on their way to a nursery specializing in roses. Rosemary has the catalogue open on her lap. When she'd got back from shopping she made a salami, cheese, and arugula sandwich, taken it and the catalogue out to the table under the plum tree, and circled the roses she liked the sound of. Getting caught up in the roses made her feel much better. In fact, if Penelope hadn't brought up the subject of mortality Rosemary would probably have managed to keep it out of her mind for the rest of the day.

"Do you ever think about death?" she asks in a voice that comes out funny, a voice belonging to someone younger and much more unsure of herself. Luckily Penelope does not notice this strange shy person in her car, or if she does, she does not say so.

"Oh, all the time. I ask myself, what if Bruce drops dead to-morrow? Or, since you mention it, this afternoon. God help us. I'll be stuck with the shop. I'd have to go in every bloody day. Well, maybe I could afford to pay someone to come in one day a week. But I ask you, one day a week to myself. Well, not even that actually when you take into consideration the account books that I'd have to keep. I keep nagging him to cut down on the drinking but he takes no notice. I try to at least keep scotch out of the house but he gets hold of it anyway. You can tell I re-late everything to drink. I mean, bugger the cheese sandwiches. On the other hand, due to months of nagging, he did take him-self off for a liver function test the other day and the results were perfectly normal. Now that hardly seems right, does it? I'm thrilled, of course. On the other hand, I was rather counting on it to give him a good healthy scare. If you know what I mean."

"Your own death, I meant."

"My own death. I see. Well no, actually. I don't think so, no. I don't mean to say I don't occasionally, you know, worry about getting ill with something terrible and painful. Cancer I sup-pose I think of mostly, though it's not the only thing, God knows. It's the bit before death that frightens me. Supposing I had a stroke and it left me helpless. No thanks. When I die I want it to be flash, bingo, all over. No dawdling round in agony, gibbering and drooling. Reminds me of my father-in-law. He hung around for ages like that, using all the wrong words for everything. I didn't like him much to begin with. By the time he was finally gathered I positively hated him. Jesus, who brought this up? Feeling a bit low today, are we, darling?" Penelope turns and stares at Rosemary intently. The car swerves slightly. "You haven't found a lump or anything, have you? Because if you have you must have it checked out immediately." Penelope slams on the brakes as though intending to turn round and head in the direction of medical assistance there and then. The car behind flies narrowly past, horn screaming. It's the closest Rosemary's been to death for a long time and she's got away with it. She laughs.

"That's better," observes Penelope, and it is.

They go on to buy roses called Marie Antoinette, Claudine, Albertine, Josephine, Ninette de Valois, and the Prioress, who, at the last minute, are joined in the back by Dolly Parton and Bob Hope who keep to themselves on the floor behind the driver, a wise decision given the present company who draw in their skirts and fall to whispering and rustling together spikily on the back seat. Rosemary thinks of the vanished Theresa, of her smashed and solemn saints.

On the way home they stop for a drink. Rosemary remembers the instant scratchies in her pocket. They fall on them with glee but not one of them proves to be any good.

"You've got to do something about your car," says Penelope. This is true, but Rosemary's putting it off. She quite likes the idea of being stranded in the mountains, or feeling as though she is even if she isn't. She also knows that, like her boots, the car she buys will probably last longer on this earth than she will, which makes her dislike whatever it is before she even buys it. Rosemary tells herself sternly that she must stop comparing her own longevity with that of inanimate objects. She can't even go into antique shops anymore without thinking how everything in them has been owned by at least one dead person. Penelope suddenly laughs her uproarious laugh, causing Rosemary's own lips to twitch.

"What?"

"I was just thinking about my above-mentioned pa-in-law. His one endearing feature was the way he used to torture us with classical music. After that first stroke he'd sit in his chair on the side verandah and he'd make these god-awful twisted sounds like, you know, rumpity tumpity honk honk blah, and he'd get furious, just absolutely filled with rage when we couldn't recognize what it was he was trying to tell us. I suppose he wanted us to play him a particular piece of music but I don't think we ever got it right. Poor old man. It was terribly sad really, I can't think why I'm laughing. It's not funny, is it?"

"Not really."

"No. But still, I can still see his little brown boots bouncing with fury. He was such a tiny man, you see." Penelope pauses. "Here's to the mad old bugger anyway," she says, raising her glass.

·

*R*osemary catches the train down to Sydney because she has to go and talk to her accountant. When the train stops at Penrith station she sees an advertisement for men's underpants by Calvin Klein and is struck by the narcissistic adoration with which the young man in the picture gazes down at his lumpy soft cotton crotch. People's backyards flash past, many containing rotary clothes hoists festooned with far less upscale underwear. Why are men so proud of their penises? I ask you. Rosemary asks you. After all, they all have them. It's not as though they were awarded for outstanding achievement or had to be earned in any way. Rosemary thinks it's a pity they can't be distributed on the basis of merit. As the prize at the end of a successfully negotiated rite of passage plus a simple written test on the rules of responsible ownership, for example. Obviously there should be a system where the owner could lose it as well. Rosemary's proposed list of grounds for confiscation is endless, or it would be if the train hadn't arrived at Central and put a stop to it.

Later, Rosemary meets Sara and Susan and they go to a concert. Rosemary is to spend the night at their place. Susan has recently bought an old Irish sideboard in some dark wood or other, but they can't decide where to put it. Fueled by a light supper and several glasses of champagne, Rosemary happily helps them rearrange their furniture.

·

*R*osemary tiptoes toward the toilet having woken at about four A.M. She hears one voice and then another, the latter raised in shrill reply. Then silence, a sharp slap, and some sobbing, impossible to tell whose. Rosemary stands wondering whether she should flush or not. She knows it won't wake them since they are obviously awake already but on the other hand she doesn't want them to know she's in a position to overhear what's just happened, whatever that may be. Rosemary closes the lid and walks softly back to her room.

Later that morning, when she goes downstairs, she finds Sara sitting in the kitchen with a cup of coffee scanning the *Financial Review*. Susan, she says, has taken an early ferry because she had a seven-thirty meeting. She pours coffee for Rosemary and hands her the cup. Under the makeup Rosemary sees a raw smudge on Sara's cheekbone. She wants to say something but equally she senses Sara doesn't want her to say anything, and would be appalled if she knew Rosemary knew. So she drinks her coffee and chats about this and that before gathering her things to go. Rosemary turns in the doorway to say a final good-bye to Sara sitting in her designer kitchen paying whatever heavy private price she's paying for whatever it is she wants, or so it seems to Rosemary who, busily counting her blessings, runs to catch the ferry and just makes it, leaping the widening gap between the jetty and the boat. She watches this gap widen as the ferry gets under way. Of course she could be wrong about everything. You never know what's up, what goes on in the shielded darkness of coupledom, no matter how well you think you know those involved. This could be married bliss she's seeing, for all Rosemary knows. A flotilla of disposed-of disposable nappies nudges the side of the boat.

Rosemary raises her eyes to the horizon, the reptilian sheen of the Sydney Opera House, the city skyline. Things look so much better, at a distance.

•

Floryan thinks it will take him every minute of the three days he has left to think up what to write in the visitors' book before he leaves. He flicks through the clamorous entries. Small hairs at the base of his neck rise at the prospect. The difficulty of his opening sentence fades into insignificance beside this more immediate literary challenge. After all, someone could be reading and admiring this the day after he leaves or even the same day and it will be months if not years before his opening sentence will be read and appreciated by anyone. A clap of kookaburras—Dot is in the habit of feeding these birds cubes of meat from the kitchen window ledge and Mrs. Black used to do the same—heralds Daphne's arrival with Dot's daughter Lois in tow. They've come to see if there is a large, light, hygienic room with several electrical outlets where Lois can set up her equipment. Rosemary's house is too small and, besides, there's her negative attitude, filling the air with bad vibes they don't need. Floryan, who has always wanted a tattoo, thinks the upstairs room at the back would be ideal. Though the room has been closed for some time and is stuffy and dusty it can be cleaned, the light is good, and there are lots of outlets and it has a bathroom attached which he supposes will take care of the hygiene aspects. He only wishes he could stay round longer and watch. In theory he supposes Daphne should apply to come to the center but all agree this procedure would take too long. Anyway, Lois's mother has a key to the place and with any luck no one need know they're there.

"You wouldn't, you know, do me one for free, like a bribe or hush money or something?" inquires Floryan hopefully. "Nothing too complicated. A Celtic circlet round the top of my arm would be cool."

"Sure," says Lois.

"Great." Floryan loves the idea of tattoos. He loves the idea of tattooing too. He reckons it must be a bit like anonymous sex. You spend time with a person. You draw a little blood. You cause them pain and then they disappear.

Daphne looks round the room in which the work will be done. She goes to the window and opens it. Fresh air pours in.

Floryan, feeling he is present at what must surely be some kind of an occasion, goes to his own room where he has a bottle of Jack Daniels on the dressing table. He fetches three glasses and then, on second thought, one for Dot. He finds Dot cleaning the bathroom and takes her upstairs where the four of them drink a toast to Daphne's dead women writers. Dot thinks it a great shame her lady in particular isn't here to see it because Edith had liked a laugh even though she didn't always show it. Dot supposes more people will be interested in a woman's body with pictures all over it than ever they were in Mrs. Black's books.

Lois, not fond of bourbon at the best of times and least of all in the morning, goes downstairs and makes herself a cup of tea. She needs to think. Something must be done to make the event stick and not simply to be seen as an isolated and pathological gesture. She wants this to be a public act taking place between consenting adults. She wants to shine this thing up, give it some wheels, send it spinning down the information autobahn.

"I shot an arrow in the air, it came to land I know not where," hums Lois to herself sipping Yunnan tea in this white woman's kitchen her mother has kept clean for so long even though the white woman in question is dead.

Upstairs Floryan stands behind Daphne giving her a bit of a neck massage.

"What is it then you want my Lois to illustrate on your body?" inquires Dot.

"The truth," says Daphne, which is true.

"You should make a video game out of it," says Dot.

•

When she gets back from Sydney, Alan's gone and now Rosemary's worrying. Perhaps he's found true love or stumbled on some different sticky fate. Weird things happen up here. Husbands run amuck. Wives are found mummified in car trunks. Children empty the family bank accounts and run away, which might be described as a wise move. Faggots turn up trussed like turkeys and scorched on impromptu bonfires built at the bottom of cliffs. Conjured by mist, goblins, geeks, and goons abound. Naturally, Rosemary thinks of the secateurs murderer who, although of course she does not know it, is rapidly closing in on his brother's Perth suburb.

Behind him are Peterborough, Ceduna, Eucla, not to mention the endless boredom of the Nullarbor Plain, where a man could and had thoroughly reviewed his sins, the chief of which, it seemed to him, had been the decapitation of the cat because, after all, it had really been his mother's cat and therefore a hopeless bit of revenge because what harm had she done? Turned the odd blind eye, been a bit absentminded, so what? And what else could she have done? Tucked him under her arm and run, that's what. But then, what would she have done for money? He could weep, really, crossing this scrubby relentless mess. He yearned for forests where leaves would close over his head and he could hide, turn feral and soft and green, shielded from trouble forever.

In Kalgoorlie, suddenly sick of relying on the kindness of strangers and the nerve-racking necessity of making quick getaways from gas stations, he busted into the back of a shop one night and emptied the till. It's been so easy to come this far—so easy it's starting to make him suspicious. He feels superstitious, strange, thinks he might be headed in the wrong direction. He slows for a stoplight in a place called Wundowie where a scrawny youth rises from the dust and proceeds to wash his windshield. The murderer raises his buttocks slightly from the seat and takes an untidily severed finger from his pants pocket. All the shears he'd been forced to use had been blunt as buggery but the last had been the worst of the lot.

Why were women apparently constitutionally incapable of keeping their tools sharp is what he'd like to know. He presses down the button and hands the finger, its band of rubies and diamonds still in place, through the window to the youth. Jewelry's a waste of time. It costs a fortune but then try selling it and they'll tell you it's worth a fraction of what you paid. But this kid might have a girl or a mum or some other kind of suitable female he can give it to. He presses the up button and the window glides upward, sealing with a firm and satisfactory thunk. He loves this car, it's smooth and comfortable. His favorite thing is the digital display that tells you what the temperature is outside. It's currently reading 94.1 degrees. It's great knowing that, out there, the drones are frying. If, he wonders, I'd had a decent car, my life wouldn't have been fucked up the way it was. If by itself, if with only, then why, perhaps, and maybe but mostly if *only*. If only he hadn't killed the cat.

This must be the longest red light in the world; maybe it's broken, he frets, maybe there's a loose connection somewhere. Who controls these things anyway? Who decides who must stop and who can go on?

On his last morning at home he'd grabbed the family cat, buried it up to its neck in the front lawn, then fetched the lawn mower and mowed its yowling head off. There's a loud howling of air brakes behind him too as the bad karma he's conjured closes in and the kid's hopping like he's on springs, pointing up the road with the disassociated digit and yelling something no one could possibly hear, until, seeing it's all too late anyway, he turns and bolts for home.

.

*R*osemary's neighbor Kevin can't make himself heard either as he stands politely at the door and cries out, "Anybody home?," which is a rhetorical question really since he knows there must be because the door's ajar and there's an electrical hum coming from somewhere. Probably a hair dryer, which reminds him of his wife and his throat involuntarily closes and opens again. These days he's able to handle these sudden gusts of grief and keep his feet instead of falling floorward clawing at his throat, lying for long dark minutes in the middle of a perfectly ordinary afternoon, his nose blocked with snot and loss.

Kevin never knows where he is with his neighbor. Her house stands empty for weeks at a time and then she'll turn up and usually others will follow so you never know what's happening. Even when she isn't there strange characters, often carrying plastic bags, let themselves in and out of the garage at will. She'd given him her phone number in the city once in case of emergency but he'd forgotten it was in his trousers pocket when he chucked them in the wash. The number did not survive and he hasn't liked to ask her for it again. Anyway, all he wants to tell her is that the night for their weekly garbage collection has been changed. The council sent round a notice to all the houses but he was willing to bet hers had blown away under a bush or been obliterated by rain so he felt obliged to stop by and tell her. Kevin often finds bits of his neighbor's mail that have drifted into his own garden, there being not many places for them to hide in the face of his detailed organization of nature. Aware he lacks a feel for it, he feels the least he can do is keep things neat. It was his wife who'd been the gardener. He fingers the tatty envelope with the damp letter inside it that he carries in the pocket of his shorts. Should he give it to Rosemary or not? He can't decide. For one thing he's opened it and read it. Well it was half-open anyway, thanks to some grubby little garden dweller's relentlessly grinding jaws. It was from a bloke called Billie who wanted to do things to Rosemary involving his fingers, tongue, teeth, tongue, eyelashes, and toes, which caused Kevin to wonder what had happened to the bloke's basic tool but then probably it all had something to do with the safe kind of sex you heard so much about. If Kevin ever had written such a letter to his own sadly now departed spouse she'd have thought he'd taken leave of his senses. He was a bit surprised Rosemary, given her age, was still interested in the whole blessed rigmarole.

"Are you there?" he calls again.

"Yes I am," she answers and goes to the door to find him, a widowed schoolboy with hands pocketed, shy brown sandals poised for flight, a brown leather case for spectacles nestled in the breast pocket of his white polyester short-sleeved shirt and all topped off by a still hopeful face hindered by a raw haircut.

"Come in," she suggests, but he doesn't, unable to cope with the cumbersome silences that often spring up between himself and this awkward woman.

He pulls his hands from his pockets, abandoning the letter because she surely would realize he's read it and he does not want to embarrass either himself or her. So he just tells her of the altered rubbish arrangements and admires her new rose-bushes as she walks with him to the gate because admiring the rosebushes is something Effie would have done. Effie had had a way with people; there'd been few awkward silences when she was around. Taking another leaf from his dead wife's book, though he should know better, he says:

"You ought to get a mailbox. They've got some nice ones at the hardware shop on Waratah Street. Shaped like an old-fashioned pillar-box with *VR* painted on the side."

"What a clever idea," she says.

"They're a bit different," something in her expression makes him add.

"They sound interesting." She touches him lightly on the arm before stepping back inside her gate and shutting him out.

.

"*I*'ve got seven tabs of A-C-I-D," Bruce murmurs into the phone. "Not in little pink pills with Mickey Mouse stamped on them, not that kiddie stuff. Proper tabs. Let's have a party. What do you say? Come on. The brain needs a holiday occasionally."

"I'll call you back." Rosemary puts down the phone. She's just seen the note stuck to the fridge by her Katherine Mansfield fridge magnet. It sort of swam into focus as Bruce reached the letter 'I'. How could she have missed it? It's from Alan. All it says is he'd decided to drive back to Sydney and go to work and thanks for a lovely time. He hoped to get up for a weekend in the near future though he expects she'll be back in town soon anyway.

The kitchen is littered with copies of the *Tattoo Revue* and *Skin Art*. She gathers these magazines and puts them on the bookcase in Daphne's room. She looks at the books lying gutted on the floor beside the bed. *The Body in Pain, Customizing the Body, The Woman in the Body, The Word Made Flesh, Fragments for a History of the Human Body,* and last though Rosemary's sure not least, *The Tremulous Private Body* pinned facedown on the carpet by its companions.

She resists the impulse to gather them up and put them on the bedside table. She doesn't want Daphne to think she's been prying. Now what?

The day is hot. The day is long. Rosemary spends much of it making preliminary notes for a paper she's had it in mind to write for some time on the matter of boys taking up so much public space. She thinks she'll call it something along the lines of "Gender and Recreation: The Politics of Play."

•

One sunny late afternoon Rosemary, Rupert, Bruce, and Penelope gather in the pretty courtyard of the latter two and drop acid. Daphne had been invited but she chose not to attend.

"Being with you lot makes me feel like a grown-up," she'd said. "You'll be having pajama parties and sleepovers next."

The thing is, Rosemary had forgotten how long a trip can

be. A tab of LSD is like a compact disc, she thinks—much as you enjoy them to begin with they do go on for far too long. At last, at 7 A.M., safely home, she squeezes and swallows copious amounts of orange juice to mop up the aftereffects and decides this trip will have to be her last. Just as her ovaries are about to cease pushing forth eggs surely her brain is running out of cells by now so she had better take care of the ones she still has. Feeling a weight of dead or deeply damaged brain cells piled like dandruff across her shoulders she turns slightly and, raising her hand to brush them away, who should she see but her friend the familiar fat policeman gazing earnestly through the kitchen window. He carries a large brown envelope that he holds up by way of salute. Clearly he wishes to gain entry. Rosemary goes to the back door and lets him in.

"It's about your car," he says, sliding glossy black-and-white photographs from the envelope and spreading them before her on the table. "I'd like you to take a look at these." Rosemary does so and there's her car, extruding like a rejected mouthful from the maw of a Kenworth truck.

"Oh God. What happened? Where is it?"

"It's in Western Australia. What's left of it. The brakes on the truck failed approaching a red light. Went straight over your vehicle. It's a write-off. So's the driver. We have reason to believe he was dealing in illegal substances. A quantity of marijuana was found in the trunk of the vehicle and a number of gardening implements were found inside the car itself. But that's not your worry."

Rosemary's not sure if it's the lingering effects of the acid or her own guilty conscience or what, but the tangled metal of the wreck writhes slightly as she looks at it. She turns the photo facedown. As she does so she thinks she hears a faint sigh and is swept by a desire to confess about the marijuana to clear the driver's name. Perhaps he has a wife, children—Rosemary threatens to pinch herself. She's not usually bothered by such things as wives and children.

"The man who stole your vehicle is known to the police in several states," says the policeman. "He was a scumbag. A real bastard." This information does somewhat relieve Rosemary of her impulse to confess and when he adds the strange information he'd found in the file, to wit that her car thief had once mowed the head off the family cat, that clinches it. But what about those gardening implements? They certainly hadn't belonged to her.

"What kind of gardening implements?"

The cop sighs, pulls a piece of paper from his breast pocket, and unfolds it. His eyes lumber down a typewritten list. "The exact nature of the implements is not specified." He stares at Rosemary over the top of his sheet of paper and clears his throat. "My own opinion would be that they were used in the cultivation of an illegal crop."

He refolds the paper and tucks it back in his pocket. He scoops up the photos and returns them to their envelope. He tells Rosemary all she has to do is to call in at the police station at her convenience to sign the final report and the matter is closed, and having said all this he leaves and Kristeva comes in, cobwebs clinging to her whiskers. She looks at Rosemary as though she had never seen her before in her life but unbends a little when Rosemary puts an egg in a saucepan and lights the burner. She tips some dry food into a saucer, scoops the contents of the barely boiled egg on top, and, as she places it on the floor, is rewarded by a smallish purr. Having completed her cat duties Rosemary wishes she too had something to eat, but what? What she'd most like is a pizza, but how to get hold of one? Probably you can't dial a pizza in the mountains. Rosemary looks at Daphne's closed door. Is she in there? She knocks. She waits. The door flings open. Daphne stands there looking vast and cross. She seems to be wearing several tracksuits at once.

"Christ, you look shitty," she says. "What do you want? Morphine I should think."

"Pizza."

"Up here? At half past seven in the morning? You sure about the morphine? It'd be a lot easier to organize. What about some bacon and eggs. I'll do them," she says, and she does. Rosemary feels a lot better afterward, especially when she finds some Sara Lee French vanilla ice cream in the freezer. She tells Daphne about her car, the dope, and the miscellaneous gardening implements.

"It was the secateurs murderer."

Rosemary hasn't thought of this, probably because of her exhausted and depleted brain cells. Daphne, however, is still able to put two and two together.

"You'll see. Everyone's fingers will be safe now."

"I hope so. I'm going to bed."

"Another busy day."

"Bug off," requests Rosemary, who has never entirely sub-scribed to the Protestant work ethic and has no intention of starting now. Besides, she can't see how plucking various scenes from your mother's mad miserable life and having them tattooed on your body actually conforms to any commonly accepted no-tions of work. And so to bed where Kristeva, delighted as all cats are when people do the sensible thing by retiring during the day, hastens to keep her mistress company.

Before Rosemary drops off she thinks about the car she will buy to replace the wrecked one. Mercifully she's too tired to dwell on the fact that any car she buys is likely to still be hurtling down the fast and fabulous freeway of life long after she herself has run out of gas. What she does think about is the fact that, had he lived, Bob Marley would be fifty too.

"No woman, no cry," she sings by way of a lullaby, but when she wakes up it's a different story. She's bleeding. But it's only been two weeks since her last period. This is it, then. Everyone knows irregularity is *the* major symptom. She grabs the phone book, gropes for her glasses, scans the relevant page, and dials.

"Good afternoon. Menopause Clinic. Can I help you?"

"I hope so," says Rosemary and takes the first available ap-pointment, which isn't as soon as she had hoped because it seems there's a lot of this going on out there and not enough clinics. Of course, thinks Rosemary, if it were men who went through menopause, there'd be a clinic on every corner and home visits, probably. She flips open the Women Who Dare desk diary she keeps up here to write down the appointed time and notes the fact that on this day in 1963 Gloria Steinem quit her job as a bunny girl, which surely makes this a red-letter day all round. Peering at the date Rosemary realizes time's marching on, the academic year is creeping closer, and there are things that have to be done.

Rosemary decides it's nearly time to leave the mountains, but first, of course, there's softball.

.

*T*he game's tied at the bottom of the seventh inning. Rosemary has no idea what happens in this eventuality except that the game isn't over and she wishes it were. The afternoon is hot and seemingly endless. The scorched oval glares and simmers and it seems they are going to have to play another inning.

Since nothing seems to be required of her at the moment she wanders a short way off and lies down in the shade of a tree, closes her eyes, and refuses to be bothered by the small black flies crawling on her face and the lines of ants walking across her arms and legs. She sleeps. She dreams fleetingly of funny little bottoms with human heads at both ends and then, super-imposed upon the inside of her eyelids through which the sun beats, comes a jumbled mural of human figures featuring a wide range of body modifications and adornments—African scarification, Japanese tattooing, Chinese foot binding, Meso-american tooth filing, Burmese brass neck rings, Sarawak lip plates, South American cheek plugs, New Guinea nose rings—

and then two drops of icy water land on her forehead and she wakes up.

A good-looking woman, in her late thirties Rosemary guesses and unmarked as far as one can tell, stands above her holding out a bottle of mineral water, its plastic body misted with cold. Rosemary sits up, takes it, and drinks.

"Thank you," she says.

"Sure," says the woman and sits down beside her. She takes the bottle, drinks, and hands it back. Rosemary has a minor crisis about drinking again from this bottle. She'd like to wipe the top of it first but feels this may cause offense so she takes a deep breath, crosses her fingers, raises the bottle to her lips, and drinks. The woman's not taking any notice anyway. She's watching the women out on the oval, dotted about in various field positions. A neat creature in white walks up to bat.

"Have you noticed," the woman asks Rosemary, "how very young these young people are?"

Rosemary, who has after all thought of little else for the last few months, can only agree. "And also," the other continues, "how practically every girl you come across these days is gay? They're pouring out of the woodwork, all these tiny dyke-lettes. And so pleased with themselves they are too. You'd think they'd invented it. Us OWLS should stick together, if you ask me."

"Us owls?" Or should it be we owls, Rosemary asks herself, though, in this heat, who could possibly care?

"Older Wiser Lesbians. We meet at the Women's Health Center on the second Thursday of every month."

There's a lot of yelling going on in the middle distance. The sprite in white has hurled her bat upon the ground and is walking off, hands on hips. Several girls are whistling and beckoning toward Rosemary, of whom something clearly is expected.

"You're up. Go get 'em." And so she does.

·

*T*hey've all been in the pub for hours celebrating Rosemary's home run that won them the game but now the last of the triumphant Tops have departed and only Rosemary and her new older wiser friend remain.

"I don't blame you," says some bloke out of the blue from the far end of the bar. "Men are awful. They're narrow, unfeeling bastards, unable to express their feelings. I don't like them either. I think I can truthfully say that all my best friends are women. Women are so much more giving. Well, I don't have to tell you that, do I?"

How did they get into this? Rosemary can't think. They hadn't even been talking to him, hadn't registered his presence.

"If he doesn't shut up," says her companion, "I'm going to thump him."

Rosemary hopes it won't come to this but it's looking like it might because he's going on again.

"I mean, honestly, girls, if I was a woman I'd be a lesbian too. No question. Men are thick boring rough and nasty bastards. I belong to a men's group. We meet once a week and do you know most of our time's spent trying to get in touch with our feelings. No wonder you'd rather sleep with women. I would. Well, that goes without saying. I'm not a pooftah or anything."

"What I'll do," her friend murmurs in Rosemary's anxious ear, "is ask him to come outside with us and then I'll hit him with my baseball bat and then I want to take you back to my place. I want you to fuck me."

Rosemary's not entirely surprised. She's been expecting something of the kind; looking forward to it, in fact. Why else, after all, would she be hanging round in a pub when she could be safe at home with a good book? *Tattoo, Torture, Mutilation and Adornment: The Denaturalization of the Body in Culture and Text,* Frances E. Mascia-Lees and Patricia Sharpe, editors, State University of New York Press, for example. Lois lent it to Daphne, who keeps insisting Rosemary read it.

"Well, will you come?" the owl wants to know and Rosemary thinks she probably will, about three times. Well, maybe twice, she amends, given her menopausal condition. But then what if she's all dry and shriveled up inside? Will she still be able to do it?

"What do you say?" the other wants to know. And what about Billie, Rosemary asks herself, and the answers come thick and fast and all along the lines of what she doesn't know won't hurt her, this doesn't count, anyway, it's not important, it's only a one-night stand besides I *need* this. "You might even say," says Rosemary, "that after all the angst I've been through lately, I deserve this."

"Does this mean yes?"

"Yes, it does." So the woman leans over and picks up Rosemary's hand. She has long thin fingers. Rosemary's looking forward to seeing them usefully employed. Then this man starts up again.

"I don't blame you, no, I don't. Not at all," he says, and Rosemary, at last coming round from her surprise at being in this situation and the working through of her short-lived though tiresome moral dilemmas, finds her voice and tells him, quietly, that actually they don't need his approval. He seems to have nothing to say to this, which is a good thing. Rosemary only hopes he'll remain quiet long enough for her to explain some things to him. For his own good. Personally, she'd prefer to avoid the baseball bat solution. And anyway, since she's started she feels she might as well go on.

"It isn't disgust with men which drives women into loving women. Women love women for their own sake. Because they want to. Not because they are reacting to anything men do. I'm sorry to tell you that men have absolutely nothing to do with it. Lesbians are lesbians because they have a desire for women. And, what's more, this desire doesn't go away because she has sex with men. In short, a lesbian is a lesbian is a lesbian."

"Yeah. Cool. I can dig it. I can. But listen, you know I'm on your side, ladies. But there's something I've always wanted to know. How do you do it? Come on, you can trust me. What do you do?"

Rosemary finds herself swinging firmly behind the bat option but apparently her companion has decided it's a waste of time and besides she's worried about the baby-sitter. So they go. The voice of the incorrigible one floats after them but no one's listening.

In the parking lot the two women start to laugh. It catches them out, this laughter. They're helpless with it. It seizes and shakes them utterly and uncontrollably as they cling together kissing and then it turns serious, or as serious as these things ever are. Rosemary eases the other woman up against a wall. She undoes her jeans and tugs them to her ankles. She notices the shoes as she moves the woman's legs apart, shiny soft brown shoes slightly scuffed, slightly old-fashioned, possibly purchased from St. Vinnie's, which is quite likely, what with her being a solo mum and all. Trucks rumble by on the highway. It starts to rain. Three boys, she thinks she'd said. Shit. Three. Boys. Whatever, she wants this mother of three as much as she's ever wanted any woman in her life. She just wishes she could remember her name. She'd instantly forgotten it in the excitement following the home run. Of course she's had plenty of opportunities, such as, "What'll you have, uh, sorry I'm so stupid with names" when she'd bought drinks at the pub, or "Where do you live, um . . . sorry, I forgot your name, so silly," or something like that but now it would be too rude to inquire, she thinks, as she slips some fingers inside her.

"Lift your shirt, lift it," she instructs. She wants to see these nurturing tits. Her hands find them. Nipple rings. Her fingers track the fine chain that connects them. Deborah. That's it, she's sure. She's surprised she found the name so hard to remember since it was the name of the head girl of her school during her last year there and who once, on one of the walking trips the school was so keen on, had invited Rosemary to share her sleeping bag because it can get cold in the bush at night and Rosemary had willingly done so, though of course nothing happened because things hardly ever had at school unlike now as Deborah, Debbie, Deb clings to Rosemary and moans encouragingly. Clearly this scene needs attention. It can't be settled here.

"Your place or mine, Debbie?" asks Rosemary, clearly made bolder in matters of this sort by the example of what Blaize had ended up doing with the woman with the Ray Bans and the powerful car stereo in that book she'd bought ages ago and finally finished last night.

"Mine."

"Say please, Deborah," says Rosemary/Blaize as the specter of the head girl raises its head again. She can't believe she's behaving like this, and in the pouring rain too, but it's nice for a change and it's okay, she can tell, as Debbie clings to her and whispers "please," and then, still whispering, "I'll be good. Come home with me now and I'll show you."

"Show me here." Rosemary twists a nipple ring hard and then harder. Debbie tugs at the elastic waist of the white linen shorts Rosemary wears. Rosemary thinks these shorts are foolish. She'd known at the time she'd regret wearing them but they were the only things she possessed that could be described as sporting. Deborah has a firm grip on these shorts by now and Rosemary has a brief vision of a little girl being helped to undress by her mother, standing first on one leg then the other in a steamy bathroom. This doesn't seem very appropriate. Shouldn't she be wearing black leather, chains, belts, whips, and possibly a peaked cap made of leather? Surely the baseball cap with *I can't even think straight* written on it that someone stuck on her head when she scored the home run is a bit silly in this or any other circumstance? Rosemary tells herself it's idiotic to be worried about what you're wearing at moments like this.

"We have to go," gasps Debbie. "I'm really worried about the baby-sitter."

"Of course," says Rosemary politely. There's always later, after all. The night is reasonably young, even if she is not.

.

I'd be worried about the baby-sitter too, thinks Rosemary when she sees her. Not at all the fresh-faced youth she'd expected but rather a stout tough truckie of a person smelling distinctly of cigarettes and alcohol who, making a curious grunting noise, brushes rudely past her in the cramped and odorous hallway of Debbie's rotting shingle cottage, slams aside the warped screen door and, crushing battalions of snails as she goes, waddles down the concrete path where hydrangeas stand in sodden ranks. Reaching the rusted Holden Kingswood station wagon parked at the curb, she gets in and roars off. Debbie trots out onto the sagging verandah lit by one dim bulb.

"Bye-bye, Daddy," she says as the Kingswood takes the corner on two wheels and vanishes. *Daddy?* "Come inside, darling," murmurs Debbie, taking Rosemary's hand and tugging slightly. There is a tremor in this hand, something helpless and resigned about its owner that is definitely going to bring out the worst in Rosemary. Who's Daddy? Who cares? Hand in hand, the careless lovers go. Down the smelly hallway where damp has got into the carpet and ancient running shoes smell like essence of boy and into the lounge room where a large dog, a Rottweiler German shepherd Rhodesian ridgeback cross to be more or less exact, crashes floorward from the black vinyl couch upon which it has been sleeping and stands glaring at Rosemary like a dragon waiting to be slain. And now, at last, the bedroom, which, unlike anything in the rest of the house— Rosemary hasn't been in the kitchen or the bathroom and she won't if she can help it because she can certainly imagine what *they* must be like—is clean, tidy, painted white, and contains but a single bed and a chest of drawers with various props laid out upon it; butt plugs, dental dams, handcuffs, and all that sort of gear plus a really terrific-looking strap-on dildo, the harness lovingly tooled in pink and black leather. Made in England, it says. Wow. What an expensive collection of toys. Clearly Deb Debbie Deborah, for she has expressed no preference, takes her sex life seriously. And so many lights. Rosemary looks in vain for a light switch. Debbie comes up behind her, circles her waist with her arms, slides her hands up under

Rosemary's T-shirt, takes a breast in each hand, and gently squeezes.

"Don't put out the lights. I like to see. I want to see what you're going to do to me." If she read this dialogue in a book Rosemary would of course be appalled but as it is, she isn't. Deborah's clearly keen to get on with it. Making agreeable noises she straps the dildo on Rosemary, picks up what Rosemary mistakenly takes to be an after-dinner mint, removes the packaging with her teeth, and proceeds to slide the condom over Rosemary's erect whatever it is because it's not exactly an erection is it and it's not a prick a dick or a cock it's something else and it's something that, as Rosemary cannot help but notice, casts a powerful shadow. In this case it casts it across the walls, the ceiling, and the neat white bed as Rosemary flicks it and moves her hips to cause it to point this way and that and up and down and round and round until Deb begs her to be still so she can complete her task. Deb looks so humble, so very very devoted and sweet kneeling there, and Rosemary would like this touching tableau to remain in place a bit longer but Deb's going to the bed where she gets down on all fours and spreads her ass because Rosemary doesn't think the words bum or bottom or behind or buttocks or arse apply in this situation. Rosemary hesitates, temporarily fazed to find the language of sexual desire has been colonized.

"Don't you want that?" croons Deb, all concern as she turns over onto her back, holding out her arms. "Come here. Don't make me wait, Daddy, come here and show your baby what you want." She probably should, but Rosemary still doesn't care about this Daddy stuff. And none of this is real anyway, is it? Not real the way the news you see on television is real or perhaps it really is as real as that at least. But not real in the way such things as losing your lover, your job, your wallet, or your teeth are real. Not real, no. Just a scene and "show me" insists Debbie and Rosemary does as a full moon rises beyond the window and Daddy's back, sitting on the nasty couch, feet stuffed into old felt slippers sharing a beer and a packet of salt and vinegar chips with the dog as they watch the whole thing on some kind of instant video-recording device Daddy's rigged up for herself. In her own way Daddy's a bit of a whiz.

·

Deb, Debbie, Deborah's sleeping now. Rosemary, who hasn't slept but's been lying still for a while now thinking of this and that, gets up, gets dressed.

She goes into the lounge room where Daddy has been re-placed by three teenage boys, the largest of whom is sobbing in a corner while his brothers play a video game. Rosemary hasn't seen these boys before due to the rule excluding male dogs and boys over the age of twelve from yesterday's game. The one who weeps sits slumped at a table with his head buried in his arms. There is a tattoo in the form of a target on the back of his neck at the point where his shaved hair begins. He wears a faded check shirt, ripped black jeans. His feet, sunk in huge and filthy shoes, pound the floor. Why does he cry? Rosemary would like to know. She is aware her curiosity has an anthropological edge. She wonders whether or not she should say hello to any or all of them, but they seem unaware of her presence. There's not much point getting involved anyway because, although she hasn't thought about it, she won't be seeing Debbie again, other than in the street perhaps, where they might bump into each other and stop briefly to inquire about each other's health, there being not much else they hold in common.

Worn out by the events of the night Rosemary creeps out into the tawdry dawn to find a world weighed down and dull with rain. She walks home thinking of the absent Billie. She picks honeysuckle growing wild in a hedge and holds it to her nose. She doesn't know what's going to happen with Billie. This morning she feels resigned to the fact that there's nothing she can do to affect the outcome. She'll have to accept whatever Billie decides. She's surprised at how calm, almost cold, she feels about it. Annoyance seems to have taken over from affection. Billie could at least have let her know she'd arrived safely at wherever it is she's gone. Hadn't she said she would, that morning after the party while some mad Maori was doing his best to disassemble the phone booth?

It somehow doesn't cross Rosemary's mind Billie might not be all right as she picks lots more honeysuckle to put in a jug on the kitchen table. The sky is lightening rapidly. The day looks less tawdry now. Raindrops turn silver on every leaf and twig. The moon's still hanging up there, though it's fading fast as Rosemary turns into her street.

.

Billie opens her eyes and sees a window on the far side of this room and, beyond the windowpane, she sees the same fading . . . fading . . . uh . . .

"Moon." The simple word tumbles stiffly from Billie's mouth. It bobs about in the dark between its speaker and the woman who sits sleeping in a wheelchair in the corner of the room. "Moon" bumps gently against the sleeper's ear and wakes her.

"Billie," cries Lorraine. "Oh shit, kid, you've given us such a fright."

"So what happened?" Billie wants to know when the doctors and nurses have gone.

"You flew off a wave and vanished. That's what the girls said. Marsha dredged you off the bottom and they managed to get you to the beach. They pulled yards of seaweed out of your mouth."

"Yuck."

"Tiny hermit crabs and crushed clam shells as well."

"Come on!"

"True. But what they couldn't do was make you wake up. They both had a go at the kiss of life."

Billie knows she should be grateful but what she really feels is embarrassed and a bit nauseous. She wants to go to the bathroom.

"I have to get up."

"I'll help you." Billie insists she can do it herself and does.

In the bathroom, her legs wobbly, she grips the edge of the hand basin and examines her gray face and ratty hair in the mirror fixed on the wall above.

There's something missing. Something's not there that should be. But what? Billie finds out after the doctor tells her she can go and they're driving back to Lorraine's place.

"Here. You must be dying to call your woman. I'd have phoned her myself to let her know but just the name Rosemary isn't much to go on."

Billie takes the phone and stares at it.

.

"If she was all that important . . . I mean if I really loved her, how could I have forgotten?"

Lorraine, rolling herself a cigarette, takes her time considering the question. At least Billie hasn't forgotten she's a dyke, which is something to be thankful for. She lights her neat cigarette. She passes the tobacco and pouch to Billie who can't remember whether she smokes or not so she decides to give it a try. It looks a pleasant pastime.

"When I was in the supermarket the other day," says Lorraine, "this old lady in front of me asked for a packet of cigarettes and the checkout girl handed a pack with a pregnancy warning on it—you know, 'SMOKING DAMAGES YOUR FETUS' or some such thing. Anyway she chucked the pack back and said she didn't want that sort. She wanted the kind of smokes that just give you lung cancer like in the old days. The poor girl had to go through all these packs to find one with the right warning on it and the queue was getting longer and longer." Lorraine's laughing. Billie isn't. "Yeah. Well. You don't think it's funny. It was funny at the time though. Must be the way I told it."

"But you didn't answer my question," Billie points out.

"No, I didn't, did I? Could be because I don't know the answer."

"Yeah. But still, what do you think?"

"You know how it is when you break up with someone and they vanish from your life. To all intents and purposes they might as well be dead, don't you reckon? I do. It's weird. Like having a cemetery on the outskirts of your mind. Perhaps your Rosemary got fast-forwarded into there by mistake when you were hit on the head or whatever happened. I mean," says Lorraine, "like Boy George says, 'One minute you can have your tongue up someone's arse, and the next you can't even communicate.' "

"I don't think we ever did that."

"How would you know? You can't remember."

Four frail faggots totter out of Cabin 6 and hit the pool. Grateful for the diversion, Billie asks what happened to the sick boy in number 4. She hasn't seen him.

"He got too sick for us to handle so they took him to the local hospital and he ... well, you know," Lorraine tells her. "His parents turned up from Queensland when he'd gone and took the body back with them for burial. There was a terrible scene in the ward. The man he'd lived with I don't know for how long, but a long time anyway, turned up and wanted him. The mum was prepared to be reasonable but the dad was vile. The lover took a swing at him across the corpse and loosened a few teeth. Dad's I mean, not the corpse's. Anyway the hospital sent for the cops and that was that. The poor bugger's buried in a bit of the sunshine state and his partner's on bail for assault. He's also HIV positive. He's a good bloke, actually. You'd like him. Maybe you should look him up when you get back to Sydney."

"Sure," says Billie, but she isn't sure because Billie's not good with AIDS. Everyone she knows is involved with someone with AIDS and if it doesn't turn up within their circle of friends, family, or acquaintances they go out looking for it, working voluntarily with AIDS organizations, going shopping for the dying, and putting up with their temper tantrums. But Billie wants nothing to do with the dying and she doesn't want to think about it either. She remembers how she felt when she went to look at the AIDS memorial quilt. It had been ceremoniously unfolded. Many thousand lives covered the floor of a vast sports stadium, each one reduced to a rectangle of shiny fabric. At her feet lay Wayne 1958–1991 much missed much loved and his entire life reduced to a piece of shiny pink fabric on which were stitched two black leather teddy bears linked together by a piece of chain. Billie thought that if she ever made a will she must remember to specifically state that under no circumstance should she be made into a quilt.

Worried this point of view may be out of place in a holiday resort for the gay and dying, Billie keeps it to herself. Lorraine beams down on those who frolic in the pool. "Salt water," she says. "Good for the Kaposi's."

.

The Dutch girl, the cousin of the boy Billie had become friends with on her exchange trip to Holland when she was at school, is in Australia. She's in Cairns and she wants Billie to join her. She's sent a postcard with a picture of coral on it and bright fish that dodge about when the card is viewed from certain angles.

Dirk sends his love and, having heard so much about you, I am looking forward to meeting,
regards,
Ulli.

Ulli has also written the name and phone number of the back-packers' hostel she's staying at.

Billie finds this card propped against her glass of mango juice on the breakfast tray brought to her by Lorraine in the morning. The card came last week but Lorraine had forgotten about it until now. Billie remembers who Ulli is, which she thinks amazing considering she still can't remember the woman everyone insists is her lover. The question, it seems to Billie, is should she or should she not try to find this Rosemary? It's not as though she misses her, though presumably the woman whoever and wherever she is must be missing her, could even be worrying about what has happened to her. In which case Billie must seek her out. If the woman got very worried she might call the police and Billie would become a missing person. On the other hand she might just write Billie off as a lost cause. There's something compelling about being lost, thinks Billie. It's a very free condition. Who knows what her relationship with this woman was like? If it had been good then surely she should try to find her again. If it had been bad then surely she was lucky to be free of it. She stares at the postcard in her hand. The fish move. Her head aches. She has no intention of going to Cairns. While she's thrashing around like Hamlet, the old blue Valiant pulls into the driveway and Marsha gets out. She clutches a bunch of flowers wrapped in measled cellophane. Her fit sarong-clad body shimmers in the heat as she walks toward Billie. Billie, nervous, watches her approach. She owes her life to this person. She gets up. Marsha holds out her flowers. Billie takes them and the two women hug.

.

"So, little Billie's leaving us," says Lorraine. "We'll have a party to say good-bye, yeah?"

Lorraine doesn't ask where Billie's going because she suspects Billie doesn't know herself, yet.

Those assembled are apparently in favor of the party idea. They include Billie, of course, and Marsha, Carmen, and also Melissa the National Parks and Wildlife officer who's taken to dropping round lately to see Lorraine who's playing it really cool this time. Napoleon the nurse is back too, with another client, and Napoleon's older sister Aviva has come for a visit with her teenage son Ben. Ben's presence makes a bit of a change round here.

"A party?" he repeats, as though he's never heard of such a thing. He has, of course, it's just that where he lives—which is on Lamrock Avenue, Bondi Beach—you'd be mad to have a party because what would happen is this: You'd ask your friends, which is fine, but then the surfies would be sure to hear about it from the girls and pretty soon every kid in the area would get wind of it and hundreds of them would crash the party and wreck the place and then the police would come and then, after all that, everyone would know where you live and what you've got and they'd all come back and rob you.

"Can I ask a few girls?" Ben doesn't know any girls round here yet, but he doesn't think there'll be a problem.

"Of course you can. The more girls the better," laughs Lorraine, taking pleasure in the anguished look this earns her from Melissa. She wants to jump her immediately but she can wait.

.

"Are you butch or femme?" Lorraine asks Billie later on while they're preparing dinner. Billie's a bit surprised at the question. There's considerable resistance to this sort of talk these days, as Billie points out.

"I know there is," agrees Lorraine, "but I'm coming out of

the closet. For years I kept the choreography, I just didn't do the dance, but now I don't care what anyone thinks. Life's too short. If you know what you want, it saves a lot of pussyfooting around, if you'll pardon the expression. Did you soak those sticks?" she wants to know as Billie starts to put together kebabs with the pieces of the satay chicken she's made.

"Yes," says Billie, who wishes Lorraine would stop being so bossy. It's like she thinks she's the only one who knows how to do things.

"Take young Ben over there," suggests Lorraine. "He knows what he wants. He doesn't spend hours of his life worrying about whether he wants to be on the top or on the bottom, do you, darling?" Ben, who hasn't a clue what she's going on about, smiles, waves cheerfully, and fires up the barbecue.

.

"*J* love you," complains Marsha as she sits with Billie on the beach. It's about eight-fifteen and a bright orange moon's rising, squeezing itself in spectacular fashion out of the sea.

"Ooh ooh I gotta crush on you," sings Billie to herself. Various moon freaks, goddess worshippers, retro-hippies, forest-dwelling ferals, and other youthful tribals ululate and fall about the beach banging drums.

"But you don't even know me," cries Billie, laughing above the din, though she knows knowledge has nothing to do with these things. She should be grateful to Marsha for saving her life and of course she is but how far does gratitude have to go?

Marsha sits and snuffles. Billie can't so much see as sense the large tears starting to roll down Marsha's face. What can she do? Get up and walk away? Well, she could, but she doesn't. There's nowhere to go really and she's leaving on Sunday anyway so she tries to find some words to make it better. "I'm not in any shape for a relationship right now."

"I don't want a relationship. I only want a fuck." If only, thinks Billie, who's heard that one before. "Well what's wrong with that?" Marsha wants to know.

"Nothing. Except I'm involved with someone else."

"But you can't even remember who she is," wails Marsha, "so how important can she be?"

"I don't know. But until I find out I don't want other stuff in my life. I don't need it." Stubborn, Billie chews her nails and glares at the moon as it scurries up the sky. Beside her Marsha sobs, sighs, and sifts sand through her fingers. Billie's sick of this. She wants to get on her bike and get going. She wants to get on with her life. She wants to finish her degree. She doesn't want to spend the rest of her life sitting on a beach or waitressing at the Loser Backstabber Cafe, Darlinghurst. No. What she wants is to make a few million and retire at forty. She also thinks she might spare a few of these millions to found a women's university on the Gold Coast that would possibly run a ghetto course called men's studies. Oh yes and she'd like to sing a bit too.

"I'm going next week," interrupts Marsha. "My leave will be up." Then Billie remembers Marsha's a captain in the Australian army. What would that be like? She'd like to ask but she doesn't want to risk further conversation with Marsha. Billie jumps up and goes to the water's edge. She hasn't been in the sea since whatever happened in it had happened. The moon lays a silver path on the calm ocean. Billie takes off her clothes and starts to swim. She goes as far and as fast as she can before, feeling calmer, she turns and swims back at a more reasonable pace. When she reaches the beach Marsha's gone and so are Billie's clothes. Childish, thinks Billie; they probably teach you that sort of thing in the army.

"Wretched girl," croaks a small feral with knotty hair and a dear little bone through her nose. Billie has heard of those forest dwellers though she's never seen one until now. "Wretched," repeats the wild child, skittering sideways up a sand dune, her laughing mouth revealing teeth of milky green, and Billie, shivering and naked, a small low wind peppering her ankles with sand, can only agree that wretched is indeed the appropriate word. With a shrill whoop, the child vanishes over the dune and a flat black shadow falls across Billie as Marsha approaches, holding out Billie's clothes.

"Stupid thing to do," she says gruffly, dropping them at Billie's feet before turning and marching away. The beach is bleak, dark, deserted as the little feral pops back up over the top of the dune, snaps itself to attention, and plays "Taps" loudly and rudely on a gum leaf. Marsha stops, turns, and screams: "I'll get you, you little bastard. I know all about you bastards living like packs of filthy animals on social security, breeding like rabbits at the taxpayers' expense, chaining yourself to trees to stop decent people earning a living the only way they know how," but she's wasting her breath because the child has vanished and the angry words stream sideways to be swallowed by the vastness of the beach.

•

The clams they'd dug from the sand at low tide were soaking in a bucket of water, extruding grit. Lorraine's going to make spaghetti alla vongole, something of a speciality of hers, for Billie's farewell feast. The party's going to be great. It's going to be fun. Ben's invited a bunch of girls he met at a bus stop yesterday to come and bring their friends too. Melissa's coming, of course. Luckily it's the night her husband, Terry, visits his mother to do any odd jobs needing doing round the old family home. He figures that since he and Melissa will inherit it one day it's worth keeping in good repair. It's a beautiful house wasted on one old woman even if she is his mother. One day he and Melissa will move in and fill it with kids, or so he dreams as he repairs gutters and plasters over cracks.

You can never tell with the ferals but, since the word is out, they might turn up too. And then there are the guests of course. They're all pretty keen. Preparations are well under way at three o'clock in the afternoon when Billie gets on her bike and takes off. She heads up the coast, driving fast. It feels good. She feels better. She's looking for a place she went to once with her mother, an isolated outcrop of boulders tumbling to the ocean. There, once, just before dark, they had watched a colony of sea lions surf in and settle for the night.

Everyone says there aren't any sea lions on this coast but they can say what they like. She'd seen them.

Billie finds the exit from the highway, follows a badly rutted dirt road to a gate leading into a field of cows. Billie opens the gate, taking care to close it behind her because she knows you always should. She rides slowly across the chomped grass and round islands of that bloody lantana. The cows take refuge in the far corner of the paddock and watch her progress with a stern collective glare. They seem about to burst into tears. The ride ends at the top of a cliff. Billie gets off her bike, walks to the edge, and looks down. The gray boulders are still there. The long even waves roll smoothly in, washing over the rocks. No perfect sleek round heads bobbing about out there, but what there is, astonishingly, given the rugged remoteness of this place, is a statue of the Virgin Mary, her arms raised in the universal gesture of blessing and embrace. Between those raised hands a rainbow arcs from palm to palm.

Billie scrambles down the cliff, rocks roll under her feet, and, near the bottom, she loses her balance and falls, sliding the rest of the way to land in a heap against a sculptured fold of the Virgin's skirt. She picks herself up and walks round to the front. Using Billie as a measure this statue is slightly larger than life-size. It faces the ocean, its face lashed by spray, the features seamed and corroded by great salt tears. She won't last long but how did she get here? Someone must have made her and brought her to land by boat. Billie wishes she had a camera because otherwise no one is going to believe her. Then she realizes she's not going to tell anyone. This lonely disintegrating Virgin belongs to her and the sea. She kneels at her feet, the waves curling at her boots, snaps a fragment from the hem of her skirt by way of souvenir and slips it into her pocket. She could swear, she honestly could, that Mary lowered one of her hands and stroked her hair lightly. Thus blessed, Billie clambers back up the cliff and rides away.

•

It's early morning, close to dawn. The party's nearly over. It's been great. Radical. Rude. Way cool. Filthy. A rave. Pick a word, any word, any one of the ever so many words limping round all ripped up and applied upside down and back to front depending on what week, day, minute, second you were born in. Whirling words for a random planet. Everyone had come, including the police, twice. The ferals had arrived at midnight, a rustle of bright rags clinging to a bulldozer they'd liberated from a clearing where ugly men labored dawn till dusk to support their ugly families by driving a road through the frail and failing heart of the forest. The ferals had all had showers and given each other haircuts. They'd done their washing in the swimming pool and hung it all out on bushes to steam in the first pink rays of the sun. The colorful clothing lends a festive air to the men with AIDS who, wrapped in blankets, lie sleeping in a podlike row on banana lounges beside the pool. Napoleon the nurse checks his charges before going to his bedroom to write in his diary, which he's neglected to do for days.

His sister, failing to enjoy the party, had claimed a headache and put herself to bed with eye mask, earplugs and two sleeping pills just after midnight feeling, quite rightly, that she had tried hard enough to have whatever fun there was to be had in what was, after all, some very alien territory indeed. Before she dropped off she wondered briefly where her son Ben had vanished to. Off tomcatting round the town with the girls, she hoped, because the Lord forbid he should end up a fairy like Napoleon. Not that she had anything against fairies, she just wouldn't have wanted to give birth to one, that's all. And Sophie, her darling little daughter, off on a weekend access visit with her father. How's Sophie getting on? Oh God, please don't let her be having a bad time. Don't let her have too good a one, either. Please let her love me more than she does her father. Exhausted by her efforts to maintain the facade of the family of Western nostalgia in the late capitalist world—for it is always a comfort to locate the time we find ourselves in, to pinpoint the latitude and longitude of blame—Aviva does the only sensible thing. She goes to sleep.

The ferals have made themselves instant coffee though there was real coffee available and Lorraine even went so far as to offer to make it for them since not one of them knew how. But they liked instant, they insisted. They ate lots of toast and jam, their hair splendid with beads, bullets, and feathers. They made themselves a nest in which to lay down their clean heads before entering nightscapes along avenues of pale nude logs rearing up in the rudest of gestures to a place where koala bears spin slowly slowly on spits splashing their sad fat down onto ground spongy with sawdust and all the while the party dykes are arranging themselves in front of the television set in Lorraine's cabin because Lorraine has a video her friend Jill has sent from Sydney. Jill's videos are reliably hot and Lorraine's been saving this one up for the party.

"Where're the Jaffas?" someone wants to know, which certainly betrays *her* age. There were no Jaffas to be had but there are six packets of Arnott's Chocolate Montes and several fat sticky green joints. There's a lot of Cascade Premium Lager in the fridge and quite a lot of Coca-Cola as well.

"Ready, ladies?" inquires Lorraine and mostly, with some slight nervousness, they are. Dora, the local vet, crosses her fingers and hopes there won't be any animals involved because if there are she'll have to leave. Billie leans against the back wall near the door. Personally, she tells herself, she can take this stuff or leave it but realizes she may not be telling herself the whole truth as she feels a familiar adrenaline surge of anticipation, not to mention an intense curiosity.

Lorraine, throwing her a wink, presses the play button.

The quality's appalling at first—well, all the way through, really, this being an ill-lit, badly miked amateur effort, a real-life situation and not a slick product aimed at the pleasure of men so no one minds, though why nobody makes decent quality porn movies for women is something Billie would like to know. She plays briefly with the idea of making them herself. She's happily driving round in a Ferrari and pearls looking for talent when her attention isn't so much engaged by what's happening on the screen as slammed facedown with its arm twisted behind its back. Billie rediscovers the love of her life while all the suddenly terrifying women around her whistle, catcall, and cheer, and then she does something she's never done before in her life. She faints.

•

"Jeez, it wasn't that bad, was it?" Lorraine wants to know. She knows it wasn't, because she'd had a quick preview of it that afternoon. She'd thought it was okay as these things go. The older woman was a knockout, sort of slightly surprised at herself you could tell, but really into it. Lorraine's brought Billie outside and parked her on the edge of a spare banana lounge, where she sits whimpering, her head between her knees. Desire is an elusive thing, reflects Lorraine, and one girl's idea of a good time may well be another girl's mug of Milo. You have to make allowances. The stars twinkle above their heads. The faggots are like a small choir producing scales of synchronized snores.

"How could she," whispers Billie, but Lorraine isn't listening. She's listening to Anthony, the man on the end of the line. That's not so much a snore as a death rattle. "Oh please God, stop it, no don't, don't let him," cries Lorraine. But he does and there's nothing she can do about it. Anthony lies there with his head flung back, teeth slightly bared, and Lorraine can't help thinking that this is what he must have looked like when he came. Hoots of appreciation, hollers of approval float from Lorraine's cabin. She thinks she can hear Melissa's voice among them. She wants Melissa. Even here, closing a dead man's eyelids, she wants her.

"What's the matter with him?" Billie wants to know.

"He's dead."

"Wish I was," says Billie. Ah, the self-centered melodrama of youth, thinks Lorraine. It makes you want to slap them and, without thinking about it too much, she does and feels a lot better.

·

Everyone's gone now—well, not quite: there's a couple of diehard dykes waltzing round Lorraine's lounge room singing along with k.d. lang.

> *You're still out there somewhere with someone you've met*
> *And I'm down to my last cigarette . . .*

they howl, rucking up the rugs and crashing into the furniture.

The body's gone, accompanied to the hospital by Napoleon, who made all the necessary phone calls, signed whatever papers needed signing, and did whatever else was required there before walking home the long way round, along miles of empty beach, howling his discontent to the wind and the waves though he stops this when he sees young Ben up ahead, surf fishing with two of the girls who'd come to the party last night. There is a man with them too, father of one of the girls. Ben introduces the girls and the father, who holds out a hand to shake Napoleon's when there is a great tug on his fishing line and he withdraws it to hold onto his catch. But both hands are not enough. Whatever it is out there is big and strong and determined to escape. The girls grab the man round the waist and Ben grabs them and Napoleon grabs him and, laughing and yelling, they wrestle the beast shoreward. It's coming, they can feel it. Napoleon tries to see round, over, or through this group of struggling people he's part of, tries to see what it is out there, but he can't. It's there though. He can feel its power whipping along the nylon line, hauling them this way and that as they struggle to keep their feet. Napoleon wonders just who exactly is trying to catch whom as they are slowly dragged down the beach to the water. Then the line snaps. Just like that. They collapse in a heap, groaning and laughing.

"Well, we gave him a good run for his money," announces the man and Napoleon thinks this is true. He briefly sees it as part of some larger debate—as something glimpsed, for instance, inside the changing shapes of clouds, something tantalizing that, exactly when you think you've got it, gets away.

"I think coffee," declares the man, "don't you? Fetch the Thermos, girls, and those curried-egg sandwiches while you're at it." He beams at Napoleon. "So you're this young fella's uncle are you? Goo'day." They shake hands and the sore Napoleon nuzzles up to this small group of humans, drinks his coffee, eats his sandwich, and feels better.

•

*L*orraine has at last had her way with Melissa and is still having it as Billie prepares to leave. Should Billie knock on the door and say good-bye? Should she at least wait until Lorraine comes outside before leaving? Even though anxious to be gone, she feels she shouldn't leave on such a sour note. She doesn't blame Lorraine for that slap on the grounds that Lorraine has had a lot of grief lately and Billie feels she should make allowances and anyway she has to admit she'd behaved like a brat, though honestly she hadn't realized the guy was dead, even though Lorraine had said he was. Anyway, she can't leave yet because she's waiting for someone to come and do something about the bulldozer that is sitting on the bottom of the pool. Occasionally it belches forth a stream of large bubbles that rise slowly, blistering the surface of the water. When they were leaving, the ferals had driven it in there by mistake, putting the thing in reverse instead of forward. It happened so quickly, hitting the edge and flipping over, all they could do was jump clear and run away. Billie, having first dived into the pool to get the number from the side of the vehicle, had phoned the contractor to tell him where his machine was, though she had no idea how it had got there.

"Youse didn't phone the cops, did you, love?" the anxious voice on the other end of the phone had wanted to know. Billie said she hadn't. "Only it's more of a family matter, you see." Billie didn't see. She was curious to find out. He'd said he'd be over with a crane and winch to get the thing out. Billie just wishes he'd hurry up or, alternatively, that Lorraine would come out so she could leave, and just as she wishes these things a tow truck comes rattling up the driveway and two big blokes heave themselves out. The elder of them rushes to the edge of the pool, howls, snatches off his hat, and stamps on it.

"You rat, you shit, you horrible little hound."

"It's me brother," explains the other. "He's driving our dad wild. He's one of them greenies and he's always stuffing up our gear. He says he loves them trees but I reckon he hates Dad more. Don't matter what the mongrel does though, Dad still sticks up for him."

"Like I told you," insists the other, "it's a family matter." He thrusts a wad of notes into Billie's hand. "That should cover your trouble. Bit of a mess. Bit of cleaning up. No damage. No harm done. Am I right?" Without waiting for a reply he jumps into the truck, backs it up to the pool's edge, and releases the chains and the grappling hooks. His son jumps into the pool and secures them.

The bulldozer hangs in midair, streaming water, when Lorraine at last emerges. She asks what's going on because she feels she has to though basically she doesn't care. What she wants most in this world is to get back into her bed with Melissa though, since Melissa says she'd better be getting home, and to that end has taken herself off to have a shower, Lorraine supposes that coping with all these mad people is as good a way to spend her time as any.

Billie tells her what's happened and hands her the money.

Lorraine laughs, pulls Billie down onto her lap, and gives her a great big kiss.

"I didn't mean it, kid. You know I didn't. It's just that you do get on my tits sometimes. But I still love you."

"Family matters," reiterates the logging contractor grimly, jumping from the truck to make sure everything's secure. "Least said, soonest mended. Know what I mean?"

"Course we do, mate," says Lorraine. "Don't we, darls?" and Billie supposes they do.

.

She's back on the road. She's going back. But when she gets there she doesn't stop, just tears past the park, past the beach, past the house because she finds she doesn't know what to do or say and even feels frightened for some reason. So she goes to her friend JoJo's flat, finds the spare key JoJo keeps under a flowerpot down the side of the house, and lets herself in. She has a bath with lots of bubbles and puts herself to bed in the spare room where she sleeps until JoJo comes home from work and starts calling to her cat Phyber Optik who is curled sleeping on the pillow next to Billie's head and wakes her when he jumps off in response to his mistress's voice.

"What a cop-out," comments JoJo when Billie finishes telling her the story, and Billie agrees it is but that's how it is and so that's it, really.

.

"It was her. I'm sure." Rosemary grabs Alan's arm, interrupting the story Daphne had told her on the phone last night about the time her mother Isobel had put a funnel-web spider in Edith Black's bed by way of a parting gesture. "Didn't you see?"

"Dykes on bikes all look the same to me," he says, sick of the subject, sorry his friend is having a bad time, angry with the little bitch who's causing her unhappiness. They have just been for a walk over the cliffs to Bondi, where they'd had lunch at Rosemary's favorite Thai restaurant before walking back.

"How's that paper going?" he asks, anxious to turn Rosemary's attention toward her professional life where, in his opinion, at her age it belonged. "The one about boys taking up too much public space."

"*More* public space, not too much. Yes. It's finished. Well, nearly," she amends, since she's still messing round with the footnotes.

"This could be a good year for you," predicts Alan, determined she look on the bright side. "Plus you've got a sabbatical coming up, haven't you?"

They are at the edge of the park now, about to cross the road. Rosemary looks left and right, but no bike; no Billie changing her mind and roaring back to her. Even if she did come back, thinks Rosemary, there'd be no place to park so she'd probably give up and go away.

"Have you anything planned?"

"Not exactly. Well, sort of. Yes. Italy for some of it, I suppose."

"You make it sound like Dubbo."

"Do I?"

He's quite right. The way she feels at the moment, the whole world might as well be Dubbo.

.

On the mantelpiece of the upstairs back bedroom of the writers' center sits a greeting card from Floryan. In it he has written, "Every body is a book of blood; wherever we're opened, we're red." Daphne wonders where he pinched those words from—he got them from his new friend Ruth Tongue who in turn lifted them from her favorite scribe but Daphne can't know this: Daphne doesn't know people like Ruth Tongue even *exist* yet.

Up in the mountains the work progresses and Daphne finds out Rosemary was right. It does hurt, especially on the back, the ribcage, the inner thighs, the inner arms, and behind the ear lobes.

"Think of those Jain women we saw on TV the other night," advises Lois. "The ones who have to have all their hair pulled out before they get to be monks or whatever." Daphne thinks about them but it doesn't help. The tiny needles nibbling at the surface of her skin raise small droplets of blood. She hadn't expected that, either. "And it's so noisy," she complains as Lois stands over her with the whining metal tattooing arm, its fine rubber veins filled with ink releasing color into the needles.

Lois draws freehand, talking to Daphne all the time, following the flow of her thoughts. Lois has given up trying to make sense of it. She just goes with the images, which are wild though Daphne is starting to talk of the necessity of words. What these words are to be and who will write them is not clear.

Every two hours they take a break. Lois applies ointment and covers the new work with protective gauze. Then she goes for a quick walk round the garden or downstairs to the kitchen for a cup of tea with Dot. Dot makes tea for Daphne too, though she won't take it up to her, refusing to enter what she irritatingly refers to as the chamber of horrors.

Daphne would like to speed things up by working at night, but Lois won't. She gets tired and anyway the light's not good enough. This is, after all, just a bedroom converted for the purpose and not a proper tattoo parlor. So every night Daphne goes back to Rosemary's empty house and Lois goes home to her mum's.

Living up here is starting to get to Lois. The weather's grizzly. The entire population looks as though they've just crawled out of the shallow end of the gene pool. She never feels safe in these country towns. Behind the facade of antique shops, tearooms, and the Paisley Parsley Cottages offering colonial accommodation lie the denuded bush blocks where owner-builders surround themselves with ugly piles of bricks thinking, perhaps, to ward off plague; hoping death won't find its way through the double garage or sneak in through the family-room window. In these desolate places born-again Christians torture their children and each firmly drawn curtain shields an overweight gun owner.

As far as Lois is concerned, she won't feel safe until she's back in town.

On the sixth night she phones Floryan and they discuss ways they can persuade Daphne to travel down to Sydney to complete the work. They also discuss what the end result of all this will be. Lois wants her first major work to be seen by as many people as possible. She wants it reviewed in the arts pages and in magazines. She wants to make a splash. For the moment, though, they agree it would be better not to mention to Daphne their plans for her body.

In any event, Daphne doesn't prove too difficult to persuade to return to town, especially when Lois points out that they will then be able to work at night using her friend Troy's tattoo parlor on Bondi Road. Also it's a bit lonely at Rosemary's house without Rosemary in it so on the seventh night she packs her bags, ready to leave in the morning.

.

Daphne, under more wraps than the Elephant Man, is helped into the train by Lois who also has to carry all her tattooing gear and Daphne's suitcase as well as her own because Daphne's too sore to do anything. When they're settled into their seats Lois notices the few bits of Daphne that can be seen are looking very pale this morning and asks if she's all right. Daphne nods and stares out of the window. Lois takes out a box of beads and starts threading them. She's making a bracelet for her younger sister. Daphne turns from the window. From somewhere inside her many layers she takes out an Arnott's biscuit tin with a picture of some native wildflower or other painted on its lid.

She opens the tin and gazes inside. She shakes it gently. There rises a sigh of a sort, a dry rustling as perhaps dried leaves would make when walked upon by a large spider, which Lois, looking up from her threading, sincerely hopes it is not.

Daphne holds out the tin. Lois puts her beads aside and peers in.

"What is it?"

"Words."

Lois can see the tin is full of torn-up scraps of paper. She scoops some out. The pieces are very dry, old. Many are brown at the edges where someone has attempted to burn them. Each scrap bears one, two, and occasionally three faded words written neatly in a round sort of handwriting, in a washed-out shade of blue ink. Lois spreads them on the seat beside her.

"My mother's words, after Edith Black tried to destroy them."

"Where did you find them?"

"In the back of that fucking umbrella cupboard. Where else?"

"Yes, but how? I mean when did you find them?"

"Last night. I biked over there. I got in the downstairs window at the side that doesn't shut properly. No one heard me. The three writers they've got there now were all upstairs playing indoor cricket. I went to the cupboard, opened it, shone my flashlight in, and right at the back, covered in cobwebs, I saw it. Well, I wasn't going to risk my arm in that lot and besides you couldn't reach the back of the cupboard so I fetched a broom and poked it out. I've always had a feeling, you see, that Mum was working on something when she died and I was right."

Lois reaches into the tin and sifts the pieces of paper through her fingers.

"How do you know Edith did this?"

"Well, I don't think Isobel would have destroyed her own work, and even if she had, I don't think she would've put them in Edith's umbrella cupboard."

"But why didn't Edith just chuck the bits away? Why put them in a biscuit tin and then hide it?"

Daphne gives Lois a quite alarming look. "Listen," she says, "it's a story. It doesn't have to be true. Personally I can think of several reasons why Edith might have done what I'm saying she did but it doesn't matter because the main thing is I've found the words we need."

Daphne gathers up the bits of paper Lois has taken from the tin, puts them back, closes the lid, and shakes it vigorously. Then she opens it again and holds it out to Lois.

"Pick some."

"How many?"

"Doesn't matter. Well, not *too* many," she adds, thinking of her suffering skin. "And don't choose. Just pull them out at random. And don't read them either."

This done, Daphne tries to empty the rest of the words out of the window but on this train they don't open so, for the time being, she's stuck with them.

.

*R*osemary's in the bookshop on Oxford Street again, stocking up on the kind of books she used to despise until she read the one with Blaize in it. She's pleased to see there are several Blaize books on the shelves. She buys them all. The young and disturbing one is still behind the till. This time, as Rosemary makes her purchases, she leans forward and says something in a low voice. Rosemary, who suspects she's been suffering slight hearing loss lately and already has it on the menopausal symptoms list she's compiling so they'll know exactly what's required in her designer hormone replacement patch, says, "What?" The word comes out far more loudly and crossly than she'd intended, so "What?" she repeats in a more reasonable tone.

"I said I really loved your video. My friends and I all have copies of it."

Rosemary has no idea what she's talking about. Can this be the onset of Alzheimer's and is she imagining things or did those youthful fingers linger slightly on Rosemary's own as they handed her her change?

.

*J*oJo's been out a lot lately, returning late if at all. Billie's out a lot too. The difference is JoJo's having a good time and Billie isn't. She's got her old job back at the cafe, university starts next week, and she's even got a few gigs lined up so what's the problem exactly? Billie walks in Centennial Park at dusk trying to work out why she doesn't feel brave and shiny anymore but what's that woman over there doing? Billie stops and watches the shrouded figure scatter pieces of paper along the edge of the lagoon. Swans and geese gather to squabble over the scraps until they realize their mistake and paddle off.

When the woman walks away Billie goes to the water's edge and picks up a piece of paper, but whatever was written there is now muddy and illegible. What had that been about? Love letters, thinks Billie, which brings her right back to her own story as all the waterbirds flock to bed on the island in the middle of the lake, the setting sun splinters against the skyscrapers of the city, and Sara and Susan pass by, taking Morgan, their standard poodle, for a walk in a gap they've found between the office and the opera.

"Isn't that . . . isn't it, you know?"

"Yes it is, I'm sure," says Susan, scrambling for her phone.

So now Rosemary knows for certain that Billie is back.

•

Daphne won't see Rosemary, though they talk a lot on the phone. She's not seeing anybody until the time is right but is reluctant to predict when this might be. She apparently has forgotten entirely any necessity she may have to earn a living. She has an arts council grant for this project but she's given most of that money to Lois, and since she's on unpaid leave from the university Rosemary wonders what she's doing for cash. Not that it's any of her business. Rosemary just thinks about money a lot, that's all. She's always found it an interesting subject.

She cannot resist asking whether or not it hurts to be tattooed. Does it hurt more than a broken heart is what she really wants to ask but who'd dare be so dumb at her age?

"Of course it bloody well does," snaps Daphne. "But you get used to it. The itching's bad, though, when it all starts to heal. I'll tell you what the worst thing is. It's the noise the machine makes. Sometimes I wear earplugs but then I get paranoid and think they're all talking about me so I have to take them out."

"What about music? Headphones. Stick somebody's *Stabat Mater* in your old Walkman. That'd be entirely suitable if you ask me."

"Hah ha," says Daphne, and hangs up.

•

*F*loryan and Ruth Tongue lie on the floor in front of the reception desk discussing the content of the invitations that are to be sent out for Daphne's unveiling. Ruth, who's heavily into this sort of thing and therefore claims to know what she's talking about, thinks Floryan must cease mulling over the discourse between narrative, autobiography, and spectacle and get straight to the point with Clive Barker's *Books of Blood*, Volume 1.

Listen, she instructs, and he does. Trust me, she insists, and he doesn't. I'll read to you, she says, and she does, skipping the boring bits:

He was one mass of blood now, from head to foot. She could see the marks, the hieroglyphics of agony. They wrote on him from every side, plucking out the hair on his head and body to clear the page, writing in his armpits, writing on his eyelids, writing on his genitals, in the crease of his buttocks, on the soles of his feet . . . and after a time, when the words on his body were scabs and scars, she would read him. She would read them all, every last syllable that glistened and seeped beneath her fingers. He was a Book of Blood, and she his sole translator.

Ms. Tongue sits a moment savoring the thought and then she wants to know what he thinks. Floryan thinks it's disgusting but he sees it may have some application. He knows Daphne won't approve but she has to realize that when someone does something as exhibitionistic and flamboyant as this, they lay themselves open to all kinds of interpretations.

"We should make a poster. No—*you* should design a poster. Do what you like, and we'll put it up all over the city. Okay?"

Ruth Tongue smiles. She rises from the floor and stretches. The uncountable number of things that pierce her gleam and jitter in the shadowless light of the tattoo parlor. She stretches out her hand to Floryan. She makes him think of mousetraps and he has to brace himself to take it. Her fingers close round his. He notices, with rising panic, her fingernails coated with steel, the lines of rivets where her cuticles should be.

"I can tell," says Ruth Tongue, "that I challenge your notions of an inviolate bounded selfhood."

"You do," agrees Floryan.

"You see," she tells him, "such notions seem nostalgic at a time when half the inhabitants of the Western world walk round filled with other people's organs, and even, I have read, the brain cells of other people's dead babies—though why not grow your own, cultivate your own first-aid kit as it were?"

Ruth's mouth opens slightly. Ruth's tongue flickers to reveal a few strategic teeth, all filed. "And there are, of course, more items fashioned from plastic and steel embedded in the human race than I have time to mention, many of which come with batteries included. Do you understand?"

Floryan nods and she releases his hand.

"I will make a beautiful poster for your friend. I admire what she is doing. She's taking language, taking something the modernists and all who followed after have made allusive and ambiguous and turning it into something that can be known and felt."

The door to the shop opens and a short man in a long coat hurries in.

"Ah. Caught you, my dear. That's good. Here's a shopping list. We're out of toilet paper, rubbish bags, detergent for the dishwasher, and the Lord only knows what else. It's all on the list. So take the car and pop up to Cole's in Bondi Junction and do something about it. Then hurry home, there's a dear, because our babies are restless tonight."

And Ruth Tongue takes the list and leaves, and Troy hurries into the studio to help Lois fill in the large blocks of color that are waiting to be filled in on Daphne's arms and Floryan goes home where he feeds his budgie, turns on the television, opens a bottle of red wine, and settles down to draw up an invitation list.

.

Impossible to think so large a crowd could ever have been so quiet but you could've heard a pin drop as Daphne descended from the roof of the Royal Horticultural Pavilion at the Showground to dangle above a thousand upturned faces. She is held within a great steel hoop. Her arms stretch upward and her hands grip leather straps attached to the top curve of the hoop and her feet move slightly apart as she balances herself and hangs above the crowd, a dark star revolving slowly, the pictures on her body dark shadows that shift and move as the hoop moves.

"Lights, light, lights," howls the crowd, and there are lights and Daphne leaps into living color hanging as she has been wanting to hang—a living picture with blood running through it. Impossible to take it all in. You will need to see the catalogue to examine the intricate detail, the finer points. You can perhaps guess at the line of spiders with attitude emerging from telephone receivers on each ear lobe, the perfect woodpile that covers the left breast. If you're into it you may sense the presence of Ruby's tongue, catch a whiff as it were of quote *napalm in the morning* unquote; witness the wan ghosts of academics in 37 A.D.—Anno Derrida—as they sift through the smoking ruins of literature or some such metaphor suited to a busted canon.

Tonight is just a glimpse, a beginning. If you're serious, in the future you will be able to see a lot more as Daphne transcends this venue with its gay and lesbian associations, its freakshow peepshow atmosphere, and, taken up by the art world, begins to tour the world's galleries as an ongoing artwork always different and always fresh as the work progresses and alters and faded favorites are reworked, reinterpreted, praised, thrashed, reviled. Daphne, packaged and shielded by her manager who will later become her husband for reasons nobody else can fathom but that suit both her and Floryan.

·

*T*he show's over. Rosemary walks upon the beach. Alone. No moon.

What else?

Something else: a happy ending, perhaps; a light at least at the end of the tunnel; a light at the end of the beach. Is it there? Is this too much to ask?

Ask and it shall be given; seek and ye shall find, and yes, there is definitely light at the end of this tunnel. It is attached to Billie's motorbike. Rosemary stands transfixed transformed swept up in light, swept up and onto Billie's saddle, and is borne along, born again, baptized in salt spray, spun away by kisses in the damp sand, and, just for a moment, all the female saints are resurrected, reconstructed round the rock pool.

The tiny virgin whom Rosemary had taken along to the show tonight for luck, though whether the luck was to have been hers or Daphne's or both—say both—finding herself in severe danger of being crushed leaps forth from the place in which she was put, hovers around like Tinkerbell, and jets off across the rock pool at the speed of light, which is close to "186,000 miles per second," as Rosemary, who always knows such things, cannot help but whisper.

"Gollah," says Billie, "now that *is* imbillivibil."

ABOUT THE AUTHOR

HELEN HODGMAN was born in Aberdeen, Scotland, and lived in Colchester, Essex, until 1958 when her family, sponsored by their local Rotary Club, emigrated to Tasmania as part of the "Bring Out a Briton" campaign. She eventually returned to England, lived in London for ten years and worked at a variety of jobs to support her writing career. These included working as a bookmakers' clerk, working in Harrods pet shop, and a short spell as a domestic cleaner. She has written for theater, film, and television in Australia and Canada. She now lives in Sydney.

Helen Hodgman's first novel, *Blue Skies,* was published in 1976. This was followed by *Jack & Jill*, winner of the Somerset Maugham Award. In 1989 her third novel, *Broken Words,* was published in Australia, the UK and the US, going on to win the Christina Stead Prize for fiction.

Her fifth novel, *Waiting for Matindi,* will be published in Australia in September 1998.